Starlight Shines for Miranda

Book five of the Starlight Series

by

Janet Muirhead Hill

Previous books:

Miranda and Starlight
Starlight's Courage
Starlight, Star Bright
Starlight's Shooting Star

and coming soon
Starlight Comes Home

(ordering   page)

Notes from Readers

I loved your books. Your series was more sophisticated (both in writing and in character development) than most. I liked specifically how you give Miranda and the characters challenges that don't have very obvious solutions. It's more like real life, not all tied up in a bow. It makes me want to keep reading them.
— *Celeste Maisel, age13, from Saratoga, CA*

I got the book *Starlight, Star Bright*. It is my favorite so far. My brother hates horses, but Loves your books, so I think you made a great accomplishment. I want you to write ten billion books. I did a report on *Miranda and Starlight* and got an A+. Thank you sooooooo much for the books. I'm looking forward to reading your future books. — *Jessica Wilson, age 9, Massachusettes*

Before I read *Miranda and Starlight*, I hated reading. Your books have changed my life. Last night I read Starlight's Shooting Star for three hours and it felt like five minutes. You have a gift; never stop writing books. — *Katherine Wade, age 11, Dallas TX*

I want to write and tell you how much I love your Starlight books. I'm 13 years old and have been riding since I was born. I can really relate to Miranda. I am going through the same things that she has with friends. I can't wait for more of your books.
— *Brooke Keeler, Age 13, Plain City, UT*

I liked your book very much. Miranda reminds me of me because I live with my grandma. Miranda was very adventurous.
— *Emma Scherry, Age 13, Sheridan, WY*

Miranda really has some current issues to deal with, a nice change for kids. I loved how the characters evolved, including Starlight. Can't wait to get into the next one. — *Fairfax Arnold,* author of *To Dance with Horses*

Starlight Shines for Miranda

Janet Muirhead Hill

Illustrated by
Pat Lehmkuhl

 Raven Publishing

Starlight Shines for Miranda
by
Janet Muirhead Hill

Published by:
Raven Publishing
PO Box 2885
Norris, Montana 59745
E-mail: Info@ravenpublishing.net

Publisher's note: This novel is a work of fiction. Names, characters, places, and events are either products of the author's imagination or are used fictitiously.

Printed in the USA

ISBN: 0-9714161-5-X
Library of Congress Control Number: 2004091096

About the Author

With a passion for children, Janet Muirhead Hill draws on her humble beginnings to depict both the joys and the struggles children face in adapting to the changes around them. Growing up on a cattle ranch in the Rocky Mountains, Janet's young life revolved around horses. Family has always been important to her, and she devotes much of her time to her grandchildren. Writing for children everywhere, she bases the many adventures of young Miranda Stevens on her experiences and those of her children and grandchildren.

Janet's novels have earned nationwide critical acclaim and nomination for several awards. *Miranda and Starlight, Revised edition* recently won a *Writers Notes* Notable Award. Janet has co-written the screenplay for a feature film based on her books. Most rewarding of all is the enthusiastic response from children who say her books have made an important difference in their lives. She treasures letters and e-mails from readers, as well as talking with fans at school visits and public presentations. She makes it a point to personally reply to each person who contacts her.

Janet edits and produces a newsletter/forum for survivors of child abuse and is an advocate for child abuse prevention. She writes from her rural Montana home which she shares with her husband and her granddaughter, Jayme. With three of her children and five grandchildren nearby, three horses, and other pets to care for, Janet's life is busy and fulfilling.

In loving memory,
this book is dedicated to my mother,
Dorothy Dale Muirhead
who passed away at the age eighty-nine
on January 30, 2004.
Mom was a devoted fan and flattering critic.
She heard each book in its roughest
form, for I read to her as I wrote.
Mom has always been an inspiration
and her loving influence
is a part of me
forever.

Chapter One

Miranda sighed deeply, breathing in the brisk morning air. It was filled with the fragrance of autumn, fresh from last night's rain. She exhaled slowly as she lay back on her horse to gaze at the deep blue sky. Her head rested in the gentle curve of his rump and the heat from his body warmed her back.

She was riding Starlight, the sleek black stallion who had become an integral part of her life. Anxious to ride before the day's festivities, she hadn't taken the time to saddle him. She wore her helmet, though. If she got caught riding without it, she would lose her riding privileges for a long time. Once the helmet had saved her from a serious head injury.

Wispy clouds sailed lazily overhead, and a magpie scolded her from a nearby tree. She guided Starlight through the river pasture to the faint trail that led up the hill to a huge rock formation, in which a cave yawned widely at the secluded river valley below. Beyond the cave, they stopped on a small grassy bench. Miranda let Starlight graze as she relaxed on his back, contemplating the wonders of her world, her life.

"A stallion is not safe for a child to ride!" The admonishment echoed in Miranda's mind.

She smiled, feeling completely safe. She shared a bond of love with Starlight that many failed to understand. She realized that if he had not become helplessly injured, his wild spirit might not have allowed her to win his trust so completely.

Closing her eyes, Miranda counted her blessings. No twelve-year-old girl in the world could possibly have more to be thankful for than she did. Not only was Starlight a permanent part of her life now, but she was also getting the family she always wanted. She would take part in her mom and dad's wedding later that morning. Though her parents had married years ago, her father had been missing for years, had even been pronounced dead by the U. S. Navy. Today, in an outdoor ceremony, they would renew their vows before moving into their new house together.

A loud whirr of wings broke the stillness! A sudden jolt bounced Miranda into thin air as the stallion jumped sideways. She slammed against the ground, flat on her back, unable to breathe. Stunned, she panicked as her body craved oxygen, but her chest would not expand. She lay gasping for a few moments until her breath returned. Rising slowly to her knees, she heard barking and another whirr of wings as a small covey of Hungarian partridges flapped and fluttered to a small juniper. Starlight disappeared over the top of the hill. As Miranda slowly rose to her feet, a black-and-white dog jumped to lick her face.

"Stop it!" Miranda scolded, pushing the shaggy pet away. "You scared the birds and nearly killed me. I don't know why Colton named you Lucky, unless it was bad luck he was talking about."

Miranda was shaky, but had no apparent injuries. She shook her head as she remembered how smug she felt lying back on Starlight, assuming she was beyond danger. "Pride goes before a fall" she had heard Grandpa say. Well, she had proved it. With Lucky at her heels, she trudged up the mountain to look for Starlight.

Colton, the teenager Mr. Taylor hired to ride his racehorses, had found the border collie puppy in the ditch by the county road. Mr. Taylor had grumbled about Colton keeping a "sheep dog" on his horse ranch, but had allowed it. He complained that it was the unluckiest decision he'd ever made. The dog had a knack for being in the wrong places at the worst times.

"Starlight!" she shouted into the early morning air. "Why did you leave me? Come back, boy!"

She walked faster as she thought of the promise she'd made to her mother. Mom had been reluctant to let Miranda go when Mr. Taylor had asked her to babysit his eight-year-old grandson, Elliot. Since Mr. Taylor would be back well past bedtime, he suggested Miranda sleep over. Mom finally agreed after making Miranda promise to take responsibility for being ready for the eleven o'clock ceremony the next morning.

"Be sure you shower and wash your hair before I get there at 9:30," Mom had told her. "I'll bring your dress and shoes, and I want you to be ready to put them on so I have time to do your hair."

Miranda quickly gave her word. Spending the night at Shady Hills would give her the chance to take Starlight out before breakfast, though she didn't mention that plan to her mother.

Mom had decided to have her "wedding" in Mr. Taylor's beautiful front yard. She had brought two identical dresses with her from California: one for Miranda and one for eight-year-old Margot. They were to march up the path in these matching peach and white frocks. Mom knew how Miranda disliked dresses, especially this long, full-skirted, frilly one. In a weak moment she had agreed to let Miranda wear jeans, and though she didn't renege on her promise, everyone knew how much she wanted Miranda to wear the dress.

"Would it be so hard for you to give your mom this one thing?" Dad had asked Miranda. "After all, it's only for a few minutes. You can change back into jeans the minute the ceremony ends." Miranda couldn't refuse when he put it that way.

She reached the top of the hill and glanced at her watch. To be showered and ready when Mom arrived she'd have to head back to the ranch house soon. Peering down the other side of the hill, she saw trees and brush with occasional grassy clearings, but no sign of Starlight. She looked in every direction, surprised at how far she could see across the valley. Roads, fields, and distant houses spread out below her. She couldn't

...didn't know how far Starlight

...paddock to the stable door and halted. She quickly dismounted and unbridled Starlight. Taking off her helmet, she ran to the front garden and stopped short. Folding chairs were filled with people, and the minister stood facing the crowd. Dad stood to the minister's left. Music was playing and little Kort, a boisterous three-year-old, was walking down the aisle toward the men.

"Psst. Miranda, come here!"

It was Mom calling from the kitchen door. She had tears in her dark blue eyes.

"Well, I guess you get out of wearing the dress after all," she said. "As you can see, it's time for you to start marching up the aisle."

Miranda suddenly felt very sorry that she would spoil Mom's plans for a beautiful wedding.

"I can hurry, Mom. Where's the dress?"

Mom pointed into the kitchen where the dress was draped over a chair. A pearl tiara and a bouquet of peach-colored roses and white baby's breath lay on the table. A pair of white patent leather shoes were on the floor.

"You don't have time," Mom said.

But Miranda had already pulled off her boots, slipped out of her shirt, and was pulling the peach chiffon over her head.

"Start marching, Margot," she called from beneath the white lace ruffles that lined the neck. "I'll catch up."

She stepped into the shoes and then picked up the flowers as Mom smoothed her hair and flattened it back with the tiara. The full floor-length dress covered her jeans, which were damp and stained with horse sweat. She looked at her father's smiling face as she marched behind Margot to her place in front of the crowd. There was a slight titter coming from the guests, but Miranda walked on resolutely, wondering why people were laughing at her. When she reached the front, she turned to see Lucky right behind her, his tail wagging. Colton got up from his chair, but sat back down again with a shrug as Lucky knelt at Miranda's side and looked out at the guests. Mom was already marching up the aisle and all eyes were on her. Miranda watched proudly as her mother glided gracefully toward them on Grandpa's arm. She looked like royalty in her cream-colored satin dress and pearl choker. Her long blonde hair was piled atop her head and fastened there by a pearl-studded tiara, adding even more height to her tall, slender figure.

"This man and this woman are here today to renew a pledge they made to each other over thirteen years ago. Each of you is a witness to this renewed commitment to the vows they made on their wedding day, and will repeat again today," the minister began. "Barrett Randolph Stevens, do you take this woman, Carey Elizabeth Greene-Stevens, to be your partner and companion from this day forward?"

When the vows had all been sealed with a fervent – and to Miranda, embarrassing – kiss, the preacher continued.

"This day is a celebration of the reuniting of a family; a man, woman, and their daughter. Miranda, has something to say at this time."

Miranda felt her face burn, for she had forgotten

about the poem she had told them she wanted to read. She had written it last week and put it in her pocket that morning, intending to memorize it as she rode Starlight. Suddenly she was so nervous she couldn't even remember how it began.

"Um, yeah, just a minute," she stammered. "It's right here." She pulled up one side of her dress to reach

into her jeans pocket for the piece of paper.

A ripple of laughter spread through the crowd. Miranda turned to face them, paper in her hand. She swallowed hard, then read in a steady, confident voice:

"What Family Means to Me
by Miranda Stevens

A family is my dream come true,
I thought it never would.
A treasure worth the world to me,
Of all that's rare and good.

It's not just having Mom and Dad
Together here with me,
Though this is like a miracle,
I thought could never be.

It's much more than a brand new house.
It's about how much we care,
Finding a treasure that was lost
Like a jewel that is rare.

We won't forget the beauty
Of this day so fair and bright,
For time will just increase the love
That's in our hearts tonight."

"Um, I didn't know what time the wedding was going to be when I wrote this," Miranda explained. Drawing a deep breath she continued:

"And one more thing I have to tell,
Our family sure has grown.
There's Grandma and Grandpa, and little Kort,
And Margot, the sister-friend I own."

Looking quickly at Margot, Miranda added, "Sorry, Mar. I just mean you're my sister, not that I own you. I couldn't think of anything else to rhyme with grown."

Miranda looked down and folded the paper, embarrassed by the silence until the crowd laughed and burst into applause. Mom squeezed her shoulder and kissed her on the cheek. Dad beamed at Miranda as he scooped Kort into his arms and squeezed Margot's hand. When the minister invited everyone to stay for the reception, picnic style, Miranda took Margot by the hand and followed Mom and Dad down the aisle. Lucky licked Margot's hand and trotted by her side. Miranda saw Laurie waiting for her.

"Miranda, where were you? Everyone was getting worried when you didn't show up. Your poor mother was about to have a coronary!"

"Oh! I didn't think what a problem it would cause. I got back as fast as I could," Miranda said. "Well, I guess if I'd left Starlight and walked back . . . , but, I never even thought of leaving him loose in the pasture with his bridle on."

"You look pretty in your dress and tiara, but you smell like a horse," Laurie said, laughing.

"Well, thanks! About smelling like a horse, I

mean," Miranda said with a grin. "I can't see anything pretty about this dress. I'm glad I got back in time to put it on, though. I'm really sorry about worrying Mom on her special day. Come with me. I'm going to wash up and put on some clean jeans."

When Miranda emerged from Mr. Taylor's spare bathroom, showered and dressed in black jeans and a blue satin shirt, Laurie was waiting.

"Do you remember my first day of school at Country View? You made three wishes. You said one of them would never come true, but it did today."

"You're right!" Miranda replied. "My first wish was for a best friend and I got you. My second wish, the one I said wouldn't come true, was for a regular family with my own mom and dad. I didn't even know if my dad was alive when I said that! I can't believe how lucky I am. This *is* a special day. And I almost spoiled it for everyone!"

The phone was ringing when Miranda entered the farmhouse ahead of her grandparents. Grandpa was carrying Kort, who was sound asleep in his arms. Grandma was looking through the mail they had picked up at the post office on their way home. Margot had stopped to play with the dogs.

"Hello?" Miranda answered the phone.

"May I please speak to Carey Stevens?"

"I'm sorry, she isn't here. May I take a message?"

"This is Lorna Schoffler-Carino, Kort's mother."

Miranda was stunned for a moment. Nobody had heard from Lorna since she asked them to keep Kort

as their own.

"Tell Carey that I'm flying to Montana in two weeks." The voice on the phone was sharp and formal. "I want directions to your house so I can stop by. It isn't hard to find, I hope?"

"Ummm. I'll have you talk to Grandma."

Miranda listened closely to Grandma's side of the conversation, holding her breath and thinking about how much little Kort had come to mean to her and her family. Mom had been his nanny, living in a mansion near Los Angeles. Lorna was a fashion model whose work and social life kept her away from home most of the time. When Lorna decided to marry a man in Italy, she felt her son wouldn't fit into her life-style as the wife of an internationally celebrated fashion designer.

"Oh, before you go," Grandma said after describing the route to their farm, "Carey told me she still hasn't received the adoption papers she sent you to sign. I wonder if they got lost in the mail. Oh, I see. All right, we'll expect you on the fifteenth."

"What did she say about the papers?" Miranda asked. "Why is she coming here?"

"She didn't say why; she just said she'd have the papers with her."

Chapter Two

Miranda gently shook Margot's shoulder. Margot's eyes flew open with alarm, scanned the room and finally rested on Miranda. Her smile brightened her pretty oval face. Miranda knew that bad dreams haunted Margot's sleep almost every night. She dreamed about her mother, and when the dreams were pleasant, waking was a disappointment as the reality of her loss flooded her memory. When she dreamt of the disaster—a boating accident in which her mother had drowned—she would be tormented all day.

"Sorry to wake you, birthday girl." Miranda said to her sort-of-sister.

When Margot had first come to live with Miranda and her grandparents, Miranda thought of her this way—a sort-of-sister that she hadn't asked for and hadn't wanted. But time had made a difference, and they were becoming good friends, in spite of their mutual jealousy. Miranda remembered how desperate she had felt when she heard of her mother's engagement to a man she didn't like. When she learned that the man had a daughter, she hoped the news would change her mother's mind. It didn't. The daughter was Margot.

"Happy birthday!" Miranda said again. "How does it feel to be nine years old?"

Lifting her head from the pillow, Margot eyed a brightly wrapped package Miranda was holding.

"There are more in the kitchen. Everyone's waiting for you to open them before we go to school," Miranda said. "Do you want to open them before you get ready for school or after?"

"Now!" Margot exclaimed, jumping from the queen-sized bed she shared with Miranda.

In the kitchen, Miranda smiled as she watched her parents hug Margot, wish her a happy birthday, and lead her to the gifts stacked on the table.

Barry, Miranda's dad, was still a miracle in Miranda's eyes. She adored him and thanked the lucky star that had brought him home in time to stop her mother, Carey, from marrying Margot's dad, Adam Barber. Adam left without leaving a forwarding address. After he'd been gone six weeks, Margot got a letter saying he would send her money and visit when he could, but since then, they'd neither seen nor heard from him.

"Look who's awake," Miranda said, as a chubby toddler entered the kitchen. "Say happy birthday, Kort," she instructed.

"Happy birfday!" Kort yelled. "Me has cake?"

They all laughed and Margot held out her arms.

Kort lunged for her with a hug that nearly knocked her over. She sat in the chair with him and let him help her tear the wrapping from the packages.

Kort was another surprise. His mother promised to sign adoption papers if Miranda's mother, Carey, would keep him. If not, she said she'd find another home for him, but she didn't want her new husband to even know the child existed. So Miranda had gone from being an only child in her grandparents' house to living with both her parents, a sister, and a little brother in a big new house on her grandparent's farm.

The call from Kort's mother worried Miranda, for she knew Mom hadn't received the promised papers. She thought of it every time she saw the happy little boy. Sighing, she looked back at Margot who was unwrapping the pair of cowboy boots that Miranda had bought for her. Margot had been riding Elliot's mare at Shady Hills. Elliot loved horses almost as much as Miranda did. And Margot, who idolized Elliot, was determined to learn to ride.

Mom and Dad gave Margot a certificate for dog obedience school and a new leash and collar. Margot was in the habit of taking in every stray animal she found, and strays seemed naturally attracted to her. Their home had become a haven for pets of all kinds. Besides Little Brother, a huge black Newfoundland-Labrador cross, there was a spotted mongrel that Margot named Splatter, two cats, a family of gerbils, and a lizard that inhabited their room. Margot faithfully cleaned cages and fed, watered, and played with each of them every day. The stately cat, Gleason, still lived in

Grandma and Grandpa's house.

"Grandma and Grandpa will give you their gifts when they come over for your birthday supper tonight," Miranda assured her.

"Oh, this came yesterday from your father," Carey said, handing Margot an envelope.

Margot read the birthday card soberly and then handed it to Miranda. A note scrawled in it said, "I'll pick you up Saturday morning, the day after your birthday, to take you anywhere you want to go. We'll have the whole weekend together, so decide what you want to do."

Miranda and Margot went to Shady Hills on the bus after school. Miranda hurried to Starlight's stall, while Margot and Elliot went to see Sunny, the mare Mr. Taylor had given him on his seventh birthday, almost two years ago. Elliot was a gifted rider, naturally comfortable on and around horses. Miranda was glad to see Margot taking an interest in horses. She'd been afraid of them at first. Starlight's hoof scraped the inside of the door as he pawed impatiently. He watched her from the open top half of the door and whinnied.

"I'm coming, boy," Miranda shouted. "If I just didn't have to go to school, I'd spend all day with you. You know that, don't you?"

Miranda saddled him and headed for the river pasture with her friends. Laurie was on her buckskin mare, Lady, and Christopher rode Queen, his tall sorrel thoroughbred. Queen's foal, Shooting Star, trotted beside them, often bounding away on some exploratory side trip, and then running back, neighing frantically for her mother. It was a sunny, late September afternoon. Some of the leaves were turning golden yellow, and the air was fresh and clean. This, Miranda thought, is the way life should always be.

When the girls went to bed that night, after a big birthday supper topped with lots of angel food cake and chocolate ice cream, Margot seemed troubled.

"You don't look so happy," Miranda said. "Are

you worried about seeing your dad tomorrow?"

"Yes. I don't want to go alone," Margot declared. "If I have to go with him, will you go with me?"

"Margot! No offense, but you know I don't like being around your dad."

"But I'll feel safer if you come with me."

"What do you mean? You don't think he'd hurt you, do you?"

"No, but . . . well, why is he wanting to do this all of a sudden? He never has before. Maybe he wants to take me away from you. Maybe he won't bring me back. He'd have to if you were with us."

Miranda stared at Margot. That idea hadn't occurred to her. What if Margot was right? Margot seemed to believe that Miranda could keep it from happening, but could she?

"Aren't you being a bit dramatic?" Miranda asked. "Your dad probably just wants to spend some time with you alone. What makes you think he'd take you away?"

"It's just a feeling I have," Margot said slowly. "I don't know him very well. All the time I lived with Mom, I only remember seeing him once. He came to the house on my fifth birthday. But he only stayed a few minutes. He and Mom got in a fight and he left."

When her mother died, Margot had been put into a foster home for a few days until her father could come get her.

"When your father came to Kansas to get you, how did he treat you?" Miranda asked.

"I think he tried to be nice to me, but I don't think

he likes kids. He acted like he didn't know what to do with me. At least he took me to say good-bye to Nana before we got on the airplane to go to Los Angeles. I thought he was taking me home with him, but that wasn't even where he lived."

"I know, he took you to Mom's because she was his girlfriend then."

"I was scared of her, at first. She was so tall and slender and pretty. Her hair was so blonde it was almost white."

"So why were you scared of her?"

"I don't know why. She was so different from my mom. I thought that since Dad liked her and he didn't like Mom, I wouldn't like her." Margot said.

Miranda glanced at the picture of Margot's mother on the bedside table. She had sandy red hair that was cropped short around her square freckled face, setting off her big hazel eyes. Compared to Miranda's mom, her mother was tiny. Margot looked a little like her, except that her oval face and slightly turned-up nose were more like her father's.

"Then Dad just left me there," Margot continued, "and I had to go to a huge school where I didn't know anybody. Nobody talked to me or even asked me my name. I hated it!"

"So when I came to California for the horse race and stayed with Mom, you decided to come back to Montana with me. Or maybe it was meeting Elliot at the track that made you want to live in Montana."

Margot grinned and confessed, "Elliot was the first friend I had after Mom died. He talked to me like I was a real person and not someone to be afraid of. Everyone else, even you, looked at me like I had the plague. I guess most people didn't know how to talk about how I felt, but Elliot did."

Elliot, who was a few months younger than Margot and in the same grade, had lost his mother to cancer, so he understood. But more than that, Elliot was just, well, real. He never pretended, and he never apologized for what he felt or believed. And he cared about people—about life.

"Do you really want me to go with you tomorrow? What about Elliot?"

"I'd feel safer with you, Miranda. You're older and you aren't scared of my dad."

"Okay, if it's all right with Mom and Dad, I'll do it. Where will you tell him you want to go?"

"I don't know. Do you have an idea?"

"When I was five, Grandma and Grandpa took me and Mom to Fairmont Hot Springs, just before we went to California. It was lots of fun. We played on the water slide and stayed in the pool for hours."

"Okay. Let's go there."

By two in the afternoon, Miranda had given up on Adam Barber. It would be just like him to break his promise, she thought. Why get Margot all upset if he didn't intend to follow through? She and Margot had been packed and ready since eight o'clock that morning, and had stayed close to the house. They would have gone to Shady Hills if they had known he wasn't coming. Miranda jumped at the sound of a knock on the kitchen door!

"Miranda, you open it," Margot said.

Miranda was surprised to see that Margot was trembling and her face was so pale that her sprinkling of freckles, which were usually unnoticeable, showed clearly.

With a sigh, Miranda opened the door to Adam Barber.

"Hello, Miranda. Is Margot ready to go?" he asked as he craned his neck to look inside.

Miranda thought he might be looking for her mother, for his eyes swept over Margot and continued to search the room. But Mom was busy in another part of the house

"Yes, she's ready. And she asked me to go, too. We're both packed."

"What? I didn't tell her she could bring someone along. I'm not made of money, you know. This is a special occasion for me and my daughter. I'm not taking you!"

Chapter Three

Miranda swallowed hard against the anger rising like a lump in her throat. It was a familiar feeling where Adam Barber was concerned. She wished she could tell him she didn't care. She'd rather be anywhere than in Adam's presence. But she knew how frightened Margot was and her protective instinct made her bold.

"I thought you wanted Margot to choose what would make her happy for her birthday," Miranda said. "She wants me to be with her. She wants someone she knows, and she doesn't know you very well."

"Don't tell me what's good for my daughter, Miranda Stevens," Adam said, his voice rising.

"What seems to be the problem?"

Miranda looked up to see her father standing behind Adam.

"I came to get my daughter. I can't afford to take two girls on an overnight excursion," Adam said, turning toward Barry.

"Good to see you, Adam," Barry said, extending his hand and smiling. "We were beginning to think you'd dropped off the face of the earth. And don't worry about the money. I'm paying for all of Miranda's expenses. She has plenty of cash with her. It should be more than enough for anything they want to do."

Adam calmed down a little and shook Barry's hand. But he didn't smile. He didn't argue, but he glared at Miranda. When they told him they wanted to go to Fairmont, he complained.

"You would pick one of the most expensive places around," he said.

"Do you need more money, Adam?" Barry asked.

"No!" Adam's face reddened. "I told Margot she could go wherever she chooses. I'll keep my promise."

It was a quiet ride down Interstate 90. Miranda tried to make conversation, but both Adam and Margot only grunted a one-syllable answer to everything she said, so she soon gave up. She stared out the window as they drove up the mountain to the Continental Divide on Homestake Pass. Giant rock formations spilled across the landscape. Miranda imagined climbing up the steep sides, exploring the crevices, and peering into the shadows.

"I have to go to the bathroom," Margot said as they passed a sign that said, "Rest Area, One Mile"

As they neared the exit, Adam didn't seem to be slowing down. Miranda waited for him to put on his turn signal, but the off ramp was looming fast and he

didn't show any sign that he planned to turn onto it.

"Margot needs to go to the bathroom, Adam!" Miranda exclaimed.

"I have to gas up in Butte," Adam said. "She can go then."

"But, I...," Margot began as they sped by the exit. She didn't finish, but leaned back and slumped down in her seat.

"I bet if you had to go, you wouldn't wait!" Miranda said. "She wouldn't have said anything if she didn't need to go."

"Keep out of this, Miranda," Adam said. "It won't hurt her to wait a few more minutes."

"How do you know how she feels?" Miranda retorted, but when she felt Margot's hand on her arm, she held her tongue.

Margot's eyes implored her not to argue. Her jaw was clenched and her eyes held tears, but she was right.

It would do no good to argue.

They were soon descending steeply, and the city of Butte spread out in the valley below them. Miranda stared at the sprawling town built on the edge of the Berkeley Pit, a massive gaping hole that was a remnant of Butte's early mining days. When they finally stopped at a gas station on Harrison Avenue, Miranda quickly opened the door and jumped to the ground. She took Margot's hand, and together they ran into the convenience store and found the women's rest room.

"That was mean of Adam to make you wait," Miranda said. "He's such a jerk."

"I should've gone before I left," Margot said. "I was so nervous I forgot."

"That's no excuse for what he did. I think he's mean and selfish!"

"Miranda, please stop it!" Margot exclaimed. "I don't say bad things about your parents." She disappeared into one of the bathroom stalls.

Miranda's mouth dropped open. She felt as if she'd been slapped and wondered how Margot could be so ungrateful.

"But you've said bad things about him yourself. I was just trying to be on your side," she said.

"Well don't. It's different when you say it."

Miranda didn't try to talk to either Margot or Adam as they continued west on the interstate. She silently fumed at Margot for turning on her. Miranda truly hadn't wanted any part of an excursion with Adam. She was here only as a favor to Margot. And this was the thanks she got! As she slowly calmed down, she remembered something her own father told her after she lost her temper one day.

"Mandy," he had said softly. "I know how it feels to get so angry. You're like me. Through the years I've had to fight my temper, because when I didn't, I did or said things I was sorry for later. Do you want to know what worked the best for me?"

Miranda remembered looking straight into his gray-green eyes, for he was kneeling in order to be at her eye level.

"Concentrating on my feelings and trying to hold them in didn't help. But forgetting about me and thinking how the situation might seem to the other person did. Imagining how they might feel always made my anger fade, because it was replaced by sympathy, or at least understanding."

Miranda tried to imagine how she would feel if she were Margot. Would she like to be reminded that her dad was a jerk, even if she thought so? Probably not. She would only feel worse about her father and herself, and maybe the person who was saying it. Her anger subsided.

"Hey, Adam, you missed your turn!" she exclaimed as she snapped out of her reverie "That's the turnoff to the hot springs, and you drove right past it."

"I know. I've got to get something first. We'll come back to it."

"Get something? Where?"

"Never mind. I know what I'm doing."

Miranda looked at Margot, who suddenly sat up

and looked at the road, then at her father, and then at Miranda. Margot's eyes were wide with fear.

"Adam," Miranda said, trying to keep her voice calm. "How far is it to whatever you have to get?"

"Not far. Don't worry about it. We'll be back to Fairmont in time for you two to do some swimming."

No one said a word for several more miles. Miranda looked out the window as they passed cattle grazing on the flat, partially flooded fields near the road. After several minutes, she saw a sign for the Warm Springs exit. She looked to her left at the long rows of one-story buildings and saw a sign that read, "Montana State Hospital." She smiled. She hadn't known what Christopher had meant when he had teased her so unmercifully the first few months she had gone to Country View School.

"You belong in Warm Springs! How did you escape?" he'd taunted.

When she asked what he meant, he had only laughed and told her to figure it out. Now she understood. He was calling her crazy because Warm Springs was the home of a mental institution. If she had known she would have said, "They let me out because they needed the space for someone twice as crazy, someone named Christopher Bergman." Miranda was glad that Chris was now her friend, and though they joked and teased, neither of them would say anything that mean to each other now. She looked at her watch. It had been almost fifteen minutes since they had passed the turnoff to Fairmont. She was getting scared.

What will I do if Adam tries to kidnap both of us?

Miranda wondered. *I'll get away from him as soon as I can and call Grandpa or Mom and Dad.*

Soon Miranda heard the faint clicking of the turn signal and looked up to see a sign: "Deer Lodge Next Right." Adam drove into the main part of town, turned down a side street, and stopped in front of a small white house with peeling paint and sagging front steps.

"You two wait here. I'll be back in a minute," he said as he got out and slammed the door.

"Miranda, do you think he's going to kidnap us?" Margot asked.

"Of course not," Miranda said. "Why would he want to?"

"I don't know, but why isn't he taking us where we want to go?"

"Maybe he will; he said he just has to get something first."

"Do you think he lives here?" asked Margot.

"I don't know. I thought he went to some big city back east."

Adam wasn't back "in a minute." After fifteen minutes, Miranda said she was going to go pound on the door and demand an explanation.

"No. Let's get out and go find a phone. We can call your parents to come get us," Margot said. "We can hide until they get here, in case Adam comes looking for us."

The girls argued about whose plan was better until the front door of the house opened and Adam came out with a woman.

"Get out, girls," Adam said, opening the passenger door. "I want you to meet Candy."

Miranda stared at the short blonde lady. She wore a pair of tight blue jeans and a red tank top that looked too small for her. Dark eye liner and mascara made her eyes look scary.

"Well, come on, get out and say hi," Adam said, reaching for Miranda's arm.

Miranda dodged his grasp and jumped down to the sidewalk. Margot scooted out behind her.

"Candy, this is my daughter Margot and her friend Miranda," Adam said.

"Ooh, I'm so excited to meet you, Margot," Candy said. "Come on in. I'm thawing out some hot dogs. You can meet my cats."

"Thank you, but we're on our way to Fairmont. It's getting pretty late," Miranda said.

"That's not what I heard," Candy said with a giggle.

"Adam, you promised Margot she could do whatever she wanted for her birthday," Miranda said. "What's going on?"

"Don't get excited. I promised and we will go to Fairmont. I just don't have the money to spend the night there. It's expensive. We'll go in the morning and spend the day. Candy is going to let us sleep here tonight."

"But we don't want to sleep here. We would have stayed home if you'd told us we weren't going to get to stay at Fairmont!" Miranda was beginning to panic.

"This is much closer to Fairmont. From here, we can get there early and make a day of it. Candy even said she'd go with us," Adam said. "Now mind your manners and get in the house. Both of you."

Margot slipped her hand into Miranda's and they followed Candy to the front door. The house was musty and smelled like cat litter. Miranda wrinkled her nose.

"There's the TV. Watch anything you want," Candy said. "If there's nothing on, you can watch a movie on the VCR."

She and Adam disappeared through a door off the small, crowded living room. Margot scooped up a cat from the floor, sat down on the couch and began petting the cat. Miranda glanced at the shelf full of movies. There wasn't anything that her grandparents would let her watch. Everything was rated "R" for Restricted. She picked up the remote from the coffee table and turned the TV on. She finally found a cartoon and sat down beside Margot.

"I'm beginning to think you were right, Margot. We should have run while we could," Miranda said quietly.

"Yeah. I don't like Candy. Do you think she's Dad's – I mean Adam's – girlfriend?"

"Seems like it. I wish I knew what they were planning. Maybe I can find out if I listen," Miranda said, looking at the closed door where the couple had disappeared.

"Be careful, Miranda. He'll be furious if he catches you spying on them."

Miranda tiptoed toward the door. When she was almost there, it swung open and Candy appeared with two plates in her hand.

"Oops!" Candy exclaimed as a hot dog rolled off

one plate. "I almost ran into you. Were you looking for something?"

"Sorry," Miranda said, "uh, where's your bathroom?"

"That door on the left," Candy said, stooping to pick up the hot dog. She blew on it, put it back on the bun, and sat both plates on the coffee table.

"Do you want a cola or iced tea to drink?" she asked.

Miranda stared at her in disbelief. "Water will be fine for me," she said.

"Cola," said Margot.

Miranda didn't eat anything. Margot took a bite of the hot dog that had not landed on the floor—at least not that they knew. Realizing that she hadn't seen Adam since they first arrived, Miranda jumped up and looked out the window.

"Adam's truck is gone!"

Chapter Four

Hurrying to the closed door, where Candy had once again disappeared, Miranda tried to open it. It didn't budge. When she pounded on it, it opened so fast she almost fell down.

"What do you want?" asked Candy.

"Where's Adam? His truck's gone."

"He went to the store to get me some things."

Miranda smelled good things cooking and suddenly felt very hungry.

"Is there anything I can do to help?" she asked, looking past Candy into the kitchen where steam rose from a pot on the stove.

"Oh, my sauce!" Candy exclaimed, running to the stove. "What a mess. It's spattered all over the stove."

Miranda found a dishcloth in the sink, rinsed it, and began wiping red sauce from the white stove top.

"What are you making?" she asked. "It sure

smells good!"

"Oh, some of my famous spaghetti sauce. I'm going to make Adam a nice salad, too, as soon as he brings the veggies."

"I hope he gets back soon. It really smells good!"

"Oh, you kids aren't going to be hungry again, are you?" Candy looked surprised and not very happy.

"Miranda?" Margot called from the doorway.

"Come on in, Mar." Miranda said. "Candy wants to know if we're hungry. I know I am."

"A little," Margot said.

"Well I have more hot dogs. You should have told me," Candy said as she went to the refrigerator.

"That's okay, Candy," Miranda said quickly. "We can wait for the spaghetti. It's Margot's favorite. Was it supposed to be a surprise for her birthday?"

Candy frowned and opened the lid to the boiling pot of spaghetti. "Here comes Adam," she finally said. "Go back into the living room until we call you."

The back door slammed. Adam walked into the kitchen carrying a grocery bag.

"What are you doing in here? You two get back to the living room and watch your movies."

"I'm afraid they guessed the surprise, dear," Candy said, putting down her spoon and stepping in front of Adam.

"What surprise?" Adam looked confused.

"Margot's favorite meal? Spaghetti? Her birthday surprise?"

"Oh, yeah, well I guess it's not such a surprise now, is it?" Adam said. "Go on, we'll call you when it's ready."

Miranda took Margot's hand. She closed the door behind them and led Margot to the couch.

"When did you tell your dad what your favorite food is?" Miranda whispered.

"I never did," Margot said. "Maybe your mother told him. I told her once when I stayed with her in California."

"Yeah, maybe," Miranda murmured.

Miranda looked for a telephone. There wasn't one in the living room. She went into the bathroom and found another door standing open. She peeked into the room. It was so dim, she had to let her eyes adjust. Heavy drapes hung over the window. Miranda found a light switch. There was a rumpled bed, and some clothes on the floor in front of a large chest of drawers. On a cluttered table next to the bed was a telephone.

"Here's your dinner," called Candy from the living room. "Where's Miranda?"

Miranda quickly flicked off the bedroom light. She washed her hands and, finding no towel, wiped them on her jeans. In the living room, she saw four plates on the coffee table. Candy and Adam sat on the couch. The TV had been switched to a football game. Miranda sat on the floor next to Margot and quickly ate the small portion of spaghetti and sauce. Her stomach still felt empty.

"I guess we're ready for cake," Miranda said when Adam finally finished and put his empty plate on the coffee table. "Do you want me to get it?"

Adam looked at Candy in surprise.

"Who said there was cake?" Adam snarled.

"I just supposed since it was a surprise birthday dinner . . ." Miranda began.

"Sorry, I didn't have time to make one," Candy cut in. "I think I have a little ice cream left in the freezer. Do you kids want some?"

"Sure," Miranda said.

Margot nodded.

But the ice cream was covered with freezer frost and was stringy and gummy. Neither of the girls was able to eat it, even after Candy made a production of putting a candle in Margot's scoop and singing "Happy Birthday" to her.

Miranda lay on the floor with a blanket over her. Margot was on the couch next to her. A glow from the street light shone in the window, and the furnace made a lot of noise.

"Miranda, are you awake?" Margot whispered.

"Yeah,"

"We've got to get out of here!"

"What do you mean?" Miranda asked.

"When I was in the bathroom getting ready for bed I heard Candy say, 'what now, Adam? When are you gonna lose the extra kid so we can go to Vegas?'"

"Really? What did he say?"

"All I heard him say was, 'Not so loud,' and then he started talking so low I couldn't hear him."

The suspicions Miranda had been trying to put down turned to panic. Putting a finger to her lips she got up. Margot followed Miranda's lead. They picked up their coats and tiptoed to the door, opening and closing it as quietly as they could. They didn't say anything until they were out on the street.

"I don't think Adam ever intended to take us to Fairmont. Do you, Miranda?"

Miranda noticed that Margot didn't often call him "dad," and she didn't blame her.

"I was thinking the same thing, Mar," Miranda admitted. "Maybe we're wrong, but I'll feel better if I can tell someone at home where we are."

"This is what I was afraid of. This is why I wanted you to come. I don't think he really planned to surprise me. I don't think they would've let us have any spaghetti if it hadn't been for you."

Miranda sighed. She didn't want to add to Margot's fears, but Adam had been acting very strange.

"You know I don't like your father, but I don't think he's a criminal," Miranda said. "I don't know what he's thinking, but he surely won't hurt us."

Taking Margot's hand, Miranda began to run. The sooner she called home, the better she'd feel.

"And just where do you two think you're going?" boomed a voice behind them.

Miranda turned to see Adam in his truck right behind them. They hadn't heard it, and he didn't have the headlights on.

"Get in!" he shouted.

Running from him was out of the question so Miranda did as she was told, scrambling up into the seat behind Margot.

"Where were you going, and why did you leave

the house without telling me?" Adam demanded.

"We were going to see if the grocery store was still open. We didn't see any reason to disturb you," Miranda replied.

When they were all back in the house, Adam made sure they saw him lock the door with a key, which he put in his pocket. The house was so old, it still had the old-fashioned locks that required a key from both sides.

"What? Are we prisoners? What do you intend to do with us?" Miranda demanded.

"No, you're not prisoners. You are stupid little kids who don't have sense enough to stay off the streets at night!" Adam shouted. "I'm responsible for your safety, and I obviously can't trust you not to go wandering around a strange town asking for trouble."

"You don't intend to take us to Fairmont tomorrow, do you?" Miranda retorted. "Why did you promise Margot she could do what she wanted when you had your own plans all along?"

"Don't sass me, you brat." Adam's face was red with rage. "I don't know why I ever let my daughter stay in the same household as you. I should get her away from your bad example and start teaching her some manners."

Miranda clenched her teeth shut on more angry words, afraid she would only make things worse for Margot. She turned to see Margot cowering on the couch, eyes wide with fear.

Miranda was wide-awake as she lay back down on the floor. She didn't think she'd ever be able to go to sleep. When she finally began to doze, she snapped herself awake with the thought, "What if they sneak out with Margot and leave me here? I've got to stay awake." After that, she fought sleep, but finally, as the room began to turn pale gray from the predawn light, she lost the battle.

"Wake up, Miranda."

Miranda heard Margot's soft voice break into her dream. She felt the pressure of a small hand shaking her shoulder back and forth until she opened her eyes.

"Adam's up and getting his pickup started. He says he's taking us to Fairmont."

"What time is it?" Miranda asked, sitting up quickly and throwing off the light blanket.

"Almost ten o'clock," Margot said. "You sure were sound asleep."

"I tried to stay awake," Miranda said, thinking she wasn't much of a protector for Margot.

"We'll get breakfast here in Deer Lodge," Adam said, as he turned down Main Street toward the interstate.

"I thought Candy was coming," Miranda said.

"She had a headache," he snapped.

They hadn't seen Candy at all that morning. Still sleeping, Miranda presumed.

At the restaurant, Miranda ordered a big breakfast and ate it all. When Margot said she was full, Miranda offered to finish her hash browns for her. At last they were on their way, and much to Miranda's relief, Adam took I-90 East. They were headed in the right direction at least.

Adam paid for Margot's admission to the pool and water slide. Miranda paid her own.

"What about yours?" Margot asked, as Adam handed her the wristband that would let her in.

"I don't care for swimming. They have a nice golf course. I'll come get you from the pool when I'm done."

The girls went into the dressing room and Margot began to change.

"Now's our chance to call home," Miranda said, peeking out the door. "Adam just left. I'm going to find a phone. Maybe they can get here before Adam finishes playing golf."

"Wait! I'm coming with you," Margot shouted, pulling her shirt back on. She watched as Miranda dialed the pay phone in the lobby.

"What's wrong?" Margot asked when Miranda hung up the phone.

"All I got was the answering machine at our house. Grandma's phone just rang and rang and rang. They must all be outside. I left a message for Mom, but it might be too late by the time they get it."

"Do you think Adam will take us home like he promised?" Margot asked.

"I don't know. He's sure been acting weird! We'll call again in a few minutes."

Miranda and Margot played on the water slide, but Margot didn't seem to be having much fun.

"Let's try calling home again," she said, after two trips down the water slide.

"Let's go down one more time," Miranda suggested. "Then we'll call after every three times down the slide."

There was still no answer, and Margot was getting more and more anxious. After the fourth try, Miranda started back to the pool, but Margot stopped.

"I don't want to go down the water slide any more. Could we eat? I'm starving," she said.

"Sure, we can eat without Adam," Miranda said. "I have plenty of money to buy lunch, since we didn't get a room last night."

"Okay. Thanks. He might not let us eat if he's in a hurry to go when he gets back," Margot replied.

As the girls entered the lobby on their way to the dining room, Miranda saw a poster on a bulletin board. "Trail Rides," it read, with pictures of horses climbing single file up a beautiful mountain trail.

"Look, this is only a few miles away. It looks like fun, don't you think?"

"Yes!" Margot agreed. "Since he didn't let us stay here last night, maybe he'll take us on a trail ride."

"If he would, it would give someone from home time to get here. Maybe we could leave another message for them."

After they ordered hamburgers, Miranda went to the phone again, Margot right behind her. There was still only the machine, but Miranda added to her messages, saying that if they weren't at the hotel, they might be at the dude ranch up the road.

They had just seated themselves again, when Adam found them. He ordered a sandwich.

"There's a place nearby where we could take a trail ride into the mountains," Miranda told Adam. "Could we go there after you eat?"

"Absolutely not!"

"But why not? We have time, and I have money if you don't," Miranda said.

"I'm not paying good money, yours or mine, to ride some old plugs that have been spoiled by tourists. I don't know why you'd want to. You both get to ride horses at Shady Hills, don't you?"

"Yes, but we don't get to ride in these mountains. We'd see new country and riding horses is fun anywhere," Miranda argued.

"The answer is no! When I finish eating I'll take you home. I have things to do."

Miranda hoped he really meant it. She wouldn't relax until both she and Margot were safely home.

As Adam hurried them toward his pickup, Miranda saw a familiar car turn into the parking lot.

"Grandma!" she shouted, breaking into a run.

"Wait," Margot called, running behind her.

Grandma saw them and stopped the car. Mom jumped out of the passenger side of the Subaru and gave Miranda, and then Margot, a big hug.

"What are you doing here?" Adam growled.

"We were concerned! We called the hotel to talk to the girls this morning and were told they hadn't checked in! Without any other way to get in touch, we came looking for them. What's going on?"

"I had a birthday party for her at a friend's house, so we didn't get here until this morning."

"I like to know when there's a change of plans," Grandma said. "Miranda knows that."

"I wanted to call . . ." Miranda began.

"I didn't expect you to worry," Adam interrupted. "They were with me! I'd have let you know if there was a problem."

"Not knowing where they are is a problem. If you ever take them anywhere again, let us know where they are at all times," Mom said.

"Aren't you forgetting that Margot is my daughter? I don't have to answer to you!" Adam shouted.

"Adam," Grandma said, "we were worried, that's all. I'm sure you kept them safe, and we appreciate you spending time with Margot. Were you planning anything else before you brought them home? If not, they can ride with us and save you a trip."

"Fine with me. I need to be heading the other direction."

Adam told his daughter good-bye and strode off toward his truck.

"Get in, girls, I'm blocking the drive," Grandma said.

"Grandma! Mom! There's a horse ranch with trail rides not far from here. Can we go?" Miranda asked as they scooted into the back seat.

"Hold on and I'll park. I want to know what you girls did yesterday and why you weren't at the hotel as planned," Grandma said. "I'm surprised you didn't call me, Miranda."

"I tried, honestly. We thought Adam was trying to kidnap us or something," and together the girls told the story.

After hearing what Margot had overheard Candy say to Adam about Las Vegas, Mom asked, "Are you sure? You might have misunderstood."

"No. I heard Candy real plain. She was talking loud like she was mad, until Adam told her to be quiet."

"I never dreamed Adam would pull anything like that!" Mom exclaimed. "I don't see how I could so misjudge anyone!" After a pause she added, "Though I suppose we could be wrong about his intentions. After all, he did bring you here today."

"If he wants Margot, all he has to do is come talk to us," Grandma said. "Of course we'd try to keep her if she didn't want to go, but legally we have no right to stop him."

"I still think he'd have taken her if I hadn't been along. Couldn't we adopt Margot before he tries again?" Miranda asked.

"I don't know how," Mom sighed. "Unless Adam agrees to it, we'd have to sue for custody. There'd be a court battle that we might not win."

Miranda looked at Margot's pale face. She looked so scared that Miranda decided it was best to drop the subject.

Chapter Five

"Margot didn't have much fun on her birthday trip with her dad," Miranda said, squeezing the younger girl's hand. "It may not be too late to go on a trail ride. I still have the money Dad gave me. It's enough to pay for all of us."

"Do you remember when we went riding over here when I was little?" Mom asked Grandma.

"I do," Grandma answered with a chuckle. "Remember how Corey didn't want to go because he said he could ride better than any of the wranglers, and all they had were deadbeat horses you had to keep prodding to keep them moving?"

"Yes!" Mom burst into laughter.

"What's so funny?" Miranda asked.

"The horse Corey was riding spooked when a pheasant flew up in its face. It jumped three feet sideways and he almost fell off. His face was white as a sheet, but he would never admit that he was scared," Grandma explained.

"The guy that was leading the trail ride told him what a good thing it was that an expert rider was on that horse. He said anyone else would have been thrown off. Corey was impossible to live with after that. But he didn't complain about a boring trail ride again," Mom added.

"Please, may we go?" Miranda asked again.

Grandma looked at her watch, and Mom looked at Grandma.

"I guess we have time if we can get started right away," Grandma said. "Shall we go see?"

Their timing was good and they were soon mingling with five out of state tourists who had already been matched up with horses. There were three horses left in the corral.

"Maybe there won't be enough horses for all of us to ride," Miranda worried.

When the wrangler came to take their money and ask about their riding ability, Grandma offered to stay behind if there were not enough horses for all of them.

"Oh, don't worry. We'll go out in the pasture and get another one, if we have to. But we do have one more in the barn. She isn't a beauty, but she's a sweet little horse. I think she might be just right for you, dear," he said as he put his hand on Margot's shoulder.

When Miranda saw the horse he was leading across the corral, her heart sank. Margot would surely feel cheated. The horse was a dingy, yellow-greenish white. She was much shorter than any of the other horses, her face was very long in proportion to her thin body and she walked with a slight limp.

"Is she lame?" Mom asked.

"Oh, no. She was born with a crooked hip. It makes her walk a little funny, but she's not in pain. She can keep up with the best of them," the wrangler assured her.

"What do you think, Margot?" Grandma asked. "If you don't want to ride her, you can ride this one, and I'll wait in the car."

Grandma was holding the reins of a handsome bay gelding.

"What's her name?" Margot asked the wrangler, as she reached out to touch the whitish horse's nose.

"Chalky," the wrangler said. "I think she likes you."

Chalky actually licked Margot's fingers.

"I want to ride her, if you're sure it won't hurt her leg," Margot said.

The sun was just setting as they returned to the stables. Salmon-pink clouds feathered the deep blue-green sky above dark purple mountains. Miranda sighed. It had been a beautiful ride, even though the pace was slow. She had seen a pretty whitetail buck bounding through the aspen grove near the beginning of the trail. Farther on, as they traversed a meadow dotted with bright yellow blossoms of the arrow leaf balsam root, a pair of sand hill cranes had flown over them, shouting their strange carrucking cry. But the view from the top of the mountain was the best of all. Miranda felt she had come home. Being high in the mountains inspired in her a feeling of both peace and awe that she never felt anywhere else.

As they got off their horses, Miranda wanted to thank the old gray gelding that had trudged up the mountain without complaint or need of prodding.

"May I brush him for you?" she asked as the wrangler took the reins from her.

"Oh, no. We'll take care of him."

Miranda doubted that, as she saw other horses being turned out in the corral as soon as their saddles were off. Their hair still held the mark of the saddle and dried sweat.

"Please," Miranda said. "I just want to say thanks by making him feel good."

"Me too," Margot declared, as one of the men tried to take Chalky's lead rope from her.

The men looked at Grandma and Mom, hoping, Miranda guessed, that they'd tell the kids no.

"We can wait a few minutes," Grandma said. "We've always taught the girls to brush out their horses. It won't interfere with your schedule, will it?" she asked.

"Well, I guess not. Get a couple brushes, Tom," he told the young man who was trying to take Chalky.

As the girls brushed out their horses, Tom and another man put saddles away. Miranda was in another world, daydreaming that she was riding Starlight over the trail they had just traversed and beyond, racing over flower-studded meadows.

"Miranda, did you hear what those guys said

about Sea Foam?" Margot asked as the two girls crawled into bed.

"Sea Foam? What are you talking about?"

"The horse I rode today. I heard those guys talking when I was brushing her," Margot said.

"Chalky?" Miranda asked.

"That's a stupid name. It's not pretty at all. You named Starlight because you didn't like his real name, Sir Jet something. I can name my horse, too."

"Your horse?"

"I have to find a way to buy her. Right now!" Margot exclaimed. "They're going to sell her for dog meat. I heard them say so."

"Are you sure? Maybe they were talking about something else."

"I know! I heard that guy called Tom say they were taking her to the sale in Butte at the end of the month. I know he was talking about her because he said, 'I don't know why they've kept the runt around as long as they have, with her crooked leg and big ugly head.' Then the other guy said, 'Max was going to load her up to take her to the sale but Charlie just had to sell one more ride.' Now do you think they were talking about something else?" Margot asked.

"I guess not," Miranda conceded. "Let's call them tomorrow. I have the phone number in the brochure I picked up at the hot springs. We'll tell them we want to buy her and make sure they don't do anything until we get there with the money."

"Thanks," Margot whispered.

"Why Sea Foam?" Miranda asked, thinking that it wasn't the prettiest name she'd ever heard.

"When I was really little, we lived near the ocean in Massachusetts. The shore was very steep and the waves crashed against the rocks. When they went out again, they left little pools in the spaces between the rocks. The water was all foamy and kind of a greenish white. Mom and I called it sea foam. It's just the same color as my horse."

"I didn't know you lived by the sea. I thought you lived in Kansas."

"We moved to Kansas when I was six. Mom's parents lived there and they weren't doing very well.

Granddaddy died about a month after we got there. I never liked Kansas. It was hot and I missed the ocean."

True to her word, Miranda phoned the next day. The man said he couldn't hold the horse without a guarantee. If they didn't have the money in three weeks it would be too late.

"How much money?" Miranda asked.

"Well, we could let you have her for three hundred," he said.

Miranda's heart sank. How would she and Margot ever raise that much money? She'd have to ask for help.

"I'm sorry, I just tied up all my money in a business deal," Dad replied when Miranda asked if he would help.

"But I thought you had lots of money," said Miranda, not even trying to hide her disappointment.

"I had enough to buy some property and build a house. Or so I thought. Mr. Caruthers is selling his ranch and I couldn't resist, even though it's more than I had saved. I put everything I had on a down payment and borrowed the rest. It's perfect, though. He has twelve hundred forty acres of fertile bottomland, and it's right next-door. Our house is close to the property line, so now I can put up some outbuildings on it and make it the ranch headquarters."

"You mean you don't have any money left?"

"I saved a little to build fences and buy some equipment at Caruthers' auction next month."

Miranda had always liked the Caruthers' Place. Once in a while her grandfather's cows escaped through the fences, and she helped round them up. She'd always dreamed of riding a horse through the lush meadows along the river. Now it was going to belong to her family! She'd just have to find another way to help Margot buy Sea Foam.

Grandpa said he was strapped after paying medical bills for his recent back injury. Grandma said the same thing. Mom said she had no savings and if she did, she had more important things to do with her money than to buy a horse! She no longer had a job and she now had three kids to support. Miranda knew that Grandpa and Dad both helped her with those expenses, but Mom worried about them anyway.

At Shady Hills the next day, Miranda waited for Mr. Taylor to come out of his house.

"Is there any work I can do for you, Mr. Taylor?" she asked. "I can clean stalls, feed, or even clean your house if you want."

"What do you want?" he asked suspiciously.

"I want to earn some money. It's an emergency and I'll do anything. You know I'm a good worker."

"I'm sorry, but I don't have anything extra. I'm paying Colton, Higgins, and your father. That's about all I can afford right now. Besides, they're keeping up with the work just fine."

Deeply disappointed, Miranda saddled Starlight and rode him to the racetrack. She avoided Margot, reluctant to tell her the bad news. Miranda fully understood Margot's feelings about Sea Foam. Even an ugly horse deserved a good life.

"Miranda!" Margot shouted from the family room as Miranda did her homework after supper. "Come here, quick!"

Annoyed at the interruption, Miranda put a bookmark in her novel and stood up.

"Oh, you missed it," Margot moaned.

"What was it?"

"The guy was interviewing a woman about raising money for the Humane Society. She had the cutest dog on the show, asking people to adopt him."

"I don't think we need any more dogs. If you ask Mom, I'm pretty sure she won't let you adopt another one."

"That isn't the part I wanted you to see. It's an idea for saving Sea Foam!" Margot said. "Listen, they're talking about it again."

A woman holding a dog was inviting people to a dance to raise money for the Humane Society. "Call the number on your screen and pledge your support. How much will you give for each quarter-hour Matt tap dances, Julie twirls her baton, or Jason does his juggling act? These talented employees of the Humane Society have pledged to perform until they drop, as you pledge your money to watch them. Help us save our dogs and cats."

"And how is that supposed to help us save Sea Foam?" Miranda asked.

"We could do something like that, couldn't we?" Margot asked. "Get people to pay money for however much time we put in? It's like Jump Rope for the Heart, or . . ."

"Who's going to pay money for us to dance in the streets to save Sea Foam? Nobody cares about us or your horse."

Margot looked like she might cry so Miranda put an arm around her. She picked up the phone and began dialing to reassure Margot.

"We'll think of something, Margot."

A woman answered the phone. Miranda explained their situation and added, "I was hoping you could take a little less than three hundred."

"They were going to charge you three hundred?" the woman asked in amazement. "They know very well they'll be lucky to get half that at the auction. I'll have a talk with them! Do you think you could come up with one hundred fifty?"

"Oh, thanks! We'll sure try. Don't let them sell her without calling us first."

Miranda forgot her worries about Sea Foam and everything else as Starlight flew around the track at Shady Hills. She felt as if they were one being, free and separate from the rest of the world. The wind in her face blew away every care, and for the moment, at least, nothing mattered except that she was on her horse, moving so fast that no worries could catch her. Then it hit her; a way to make the money to save Sea Foam. She guided Starlight through the gate to the racetrack and galloped toward the house. Mr. Taylor was walking to his garage.

"Mr. Taylor," Miranda called as he opened the garage door.

She brought Starlight to an abrupt stop as he stared at her in surprise. He was getting old, Miranda suddenly realized, as she saw how stooped his back was getting as he held on to the door for support. She swung off Starlight and jumped to the ground.

"I have the most wonderful idea, Mr. Taylor. It'll help both of us. We can have a race! Here. On your track."

Mr. Taylor stared at her in confusion.

"What kind of fool scheme are you brewing up this time?" he asked.

"It's not foolish," Miranda said with a smile. "It's brilliant. You timed him when I was riding, remember? You said I could get more speed out of him than anyone. You said he's the fastest horse you've ever seen. He could win . . ."

"Dumbest idea I ever heard!" Mr. Taylor declared.

"What do you mean?" Miranda challenged. "What's wrong with it?"

"First of all, no one would enter. Secondly, I'd be liable if anyone got hurt. It could cost me a bundle."

"No, that's not what I mean. Just run Starlight against the clock. We get people to pledge money on every one-fifth second he beats the Kentucky Derby winners."

"Which Kentucky Derby winners?"

"I've got all the times for the winners of the last ten races in a report I did for English last year. I'll average them and we'll use that time."

"Your family isn't going to let you ride in a race, so how is it going to help you?"

"I can talk my dad into it since I won't be running in a crowd of horses," Miranda said. "Please?"

"And you think you can get people to give you money for riding your horse around a racetrack?" Mr. Taylor asked. "I don't think so."

"Sounds like a good idea to me," came a voice from behind Miranda. She turned to see Higgins, the old groom who had worked most of his life for Mr. Taylor. Winking at Miranda, he continued: "I don't see how you could lose with Miranda riding Starlight."

"If I get people to pledge, may I do it?" Miranda asked.

"That's a mighty big if," Mr. Taylor said, "so why not? If you can get people to sign, I'll let you have all the money you raise. It won't be much."

"Thanks, Higgins!" Miranda said, grinning. "Thanks, Mr. Taylor."

Miranda could hardly wait to get home and tell Margot the good news. Margot hadn't come to Shady Hills because she had a dental appointment that Saturday morning. Mom picked Miranda up when she brought Margot back from Bozeman. The girls went to their room as soon as they got home and took out paper and markers to make a sign to announce the race.

As they stretched out on the floor to begin, Margot's puppy began barking wildly outside and Little Brother jumped from the bed, ran to the door, and scratched to get out.

"Someone's here, Mom. Wow! Look at that car!" Miranda exclaimed as she let Little Brother out.

"It must be Lorna," Mom said. "She's early! I wasn't expecting her until tomorrow."

Chapter Six

A loud, long honk sounded from the sleek sports car in their driveway. Miranda started out the door, with Mom at her heels. Before Miranda could get to the car, the window rolled down two inches and the red-haired woman inside yelled, "Get these brutes away from my car! I didn't know I was going to be attacked!"

"Little Brother, Splatter, come here!" Miranda commanded. "Margot, help me."

Soon the girls had the dogs by their collars and were leading them to a nearby shed. *"We need to work on dog obedience!"* Miranda thought. They shut them inside and hurried back to the house. They were as anxious as Mom to hear what Kort's mother had to say. When they entered the living room, Lorna was trying to hold Kort in her arms, but he kicked and cried as he reached for Mom, holding both arms out to her.

"Don't take offense, Lorna," Mom said, as she

took him back into her arms. He snuggled against her and looked sideways at the stranger who had snatched him up from where he'd been playing. "He hasn't had a chance to know you. Babies forget people when they don't see them for a while."

"Yes, I know. I shouldn't have grabbed him. I was just so happy to see him," Lorna said. "I can't believe how much he has grown."

"Will you be staying long?" Mom asked. "We have a spare bedroom, all made up, if you'd like to spend the night."

Lorna looked around their tidy, spacious living room, and shook her head. Miranda supposed it looked like a tiny shack compared to the mansions Lorna Shoffler-Carino was used to living in.

"I had to see Kort before I signed the adoption papers."

"Is there a problem?" Mom asked.

Lorna didn't answer for a long time, and Miranda held her breath. She couldn't imagine having Kort taken from their home. He would hate it. He loved every one of them, and he didn't know this woman. She had never spent much time with him, even when he was a baby. Miranda was about to say so, for she couldn't stand the silence any longer, when Lorna finally shook her head and answered.

"I'm sorry," she said softly. "I just can't do it. What kind of mother gives her child away? I promised to let you adopt him because I was afraid of what my fiancé would say if he found out I had a baby. That isn't an issue anymore, because I'm getting a divorce. I need my baby right now. And I can provide for him. I'm getting my home in L.A. back and a fair share of Carino's money."

Miranda was stunned. She couldn't breathe. Mom must have been just as shocked, for she didn't say anything for a long time.

Kort squirmed down from Mom's lap, picked up a book and held his hands up to Miranda.

"Manda wead," he said.

"But he's happy here! We don't have a mansion, but we can give him a stable and peaceful life," Mom pled. "Have you thought this through? What about your career?"

"I've thought of that. I'm taking some time off right now. I'll take Kort and see how it goes. We need time to bond."

"When?" Mom asked, blinking back tears.

"Now," Lorna said.

"But don't you think you should visit a few times first?" Mom asked. "Let him get to know you, so the change won't be so hard on him!"

"I'll be in California," Lorna said, her voice edged with anger. "I can't drop in every day. Please pack his clothes. We have a plane to catch!"

The whole family seemed numb with pain. Miranda couldn't eat. She cried herself to sleep at night. Mom let the girls stay home from school the rest of the week. Every time Miranda thought of Kort, remembering how he cried and screamed, holding out his arms to her when his mother buckled him into her car, she burst into tears. Margot handled it differently. She closed herself off, becoming quiet and sullen, just like she had after her mother died.

But they couldn't avoid school forever, and they still had to save Sea Foam. With heavy hearts, they returned to school.

Miranda couldn't concentrate on schoolwork. She thought of how lonely it was without Kort at the breakfast table that morning. She blinked back tears. Margot wasn't making it any easier. Miranda knew Margot missed little Kort as much as she did, but instead of talking about it, she just went on and on about how time was running out for Sea Foam. Well, it was, but Miranda didn't know what to do about it.

Staring out the classroom window, Miranda watched the weather turn cloudy, cold and windy, as if to match her mood. At lunch, Laurie and Christopher listened sympathetically as Miranda told them about Lorna taking Kort away.

"Jeez, what a mean thing to do!" Chris said. "He probably thinks you've abandoned him."

"Thanks a lot, Chris," Miranda said. "That's just what I needed to hear. Don't you think I've thought about that?"

"Sorry. I didn't mean . . . I just meant what a terrible mother to do that to him."

"I'm so sorry, Miranda. I can only imagine how you must feel," Laurie said, putting her hand on Miranda's. "That must be what's bothering Margot, too. She walks around like a rain cloud about to burst!"

"Yeah, plus she's worried about her horse."

"Margot has a horse?" Chris asked.

"No, but she's trying to save one. It isn't her horse, but she loves it and wants it to be hers. She even renamed it like I did with Starlight."

"Where is this horse? What's wrong with it?" Laurie asked.

Miranda told them the whole story of Chalky, alias Sea Foam.

"Margot gave me an idea of how to raise the money. There's a lady at the ranch who's trying to keep the men from selling Sea Foam until we can buy her."

"What was your idea?" Laurie asked.

Miranda explained their plan, adding, "Mr. Taylor said we can use his track if we get pledges, but he doesn't think anyone will sign up."

"I do!" Laurie exclaimed. "I think people will really go for it."

"Really?" Miranda said.

"I think so too," Chris said. "It would be something different, and there isn't much else going on right now. And people are going to think they can't lose, so they'll probably bet a lot."

"I hope you're right."

"We'll help you make announcements and pass them out and sign people up," Laurie offered. "Won't we, Chris?"

"Sure, it'll be fun."

"Come to my house after school then. We can finish the posters tonight and pass them out tomorrow."

By the time school was out, it was raining and it felt like it would turn to snow. Miranda was heading for the buses when Chris stopped her.

"Mom won't let me come over this afternoon because of the storm. Maybe tomorrow."

"Miranda," Laurie called. "Mom just came to pick me up. I can't come today. But maybe tomorrow."

Margot caught up with Miranda and the two girls ran to the bus. Miranda wished she had worn her jacket to school. The large drops that pelted her bare arms stung. By the time they arrived home, the rain had turned to large white flakes. The girls ran to the old farmhouse where Grandma and Grandpa lived, for it was closer than the new one Dad had built on the edge of Grandpa's property.

"Well, look what the wind blew in," Grandma said with a smile, stopping her work in the kitchen to hand them a towel. "I'm so glad to see you. This is turning into a blizzard. My only wish in bad weather is to have all my family safely at home."

Miranda telephoned her mother to tell her they were safe and would stay at Grandma's for a while, for already the blowing snow obscured the view of the new house that stood only two hundred yards away.

"Margot, what's wrong?" Miranda asked as she hung up the phone.

Margot stared out the window and tears rolled down her face. To Miranda the storm was exciting and she could hardly wait to go out and play in the snow.

"Now I'll never get Sea Foam! She'll be killed and I wanted so badly to save her," Margot said with a catch in her voice as she tried not to cry.

"What makes you think that?"

"Duh, Miranda! With snow on the racetrack, we won't have any way to make money. They aren't going to keep her when they have to buy hay, are they?"

"You're not used to Montana. The weather can change a lot in two weeks," Miranda said.

Grandma came out of the bedroom and handed them dry clothes.

"I guess it's a good thing you leave your clothes behind when you sleep over," she said with a smile. "Now you can change into something dry."

The storm didn't let up. Grandpa went with Miranda to feed her bunnies and chickens and shut them up for the night. She walked on to the barn with him, holding his hand to keep from getting separated, and helped with the milking and feeding. When they were done, she couldn't see the house for the blowing snow. It was very dark. Grandpa took her hand.

"I can't even see where the house is, Grandpa," Miranda said. "Why don't they have the lights on?"

"I'm sure they do. By the time we get to the garage, we'll be able to see them."

With wind stinging her face, Miranda trotted beside Grandpa, gripping his hand for dear life. He pulled her into the shelter of the garage.

"We're halfway; see the lights from the house now?" Grandpa asked.

Miranda strained to see the faint yellow glow in the curtain of snow.

"Ready to run for it?" Grandpa asked.

Miranda nodded. She wondered why Grandma didn't turn on the outside light, but as they neared the

back door, she saw that it was on. The snow was like a big lamp shade keeping the light from shining very far.

Grandma had supper ready and Margot was setting the table. A warm fire burned in the old potbelly stove in the living room. Miranda sighed contentedly. Starlight would be eating hay in his stall, and so would Queen and Shooting Star. All was well in her world, where shelter protected her loved ones – both animals and people – from a raging blizzard.

By bedtime, the wind was still whistling through the cracks in the window casing, and Grandma told the girls to sleep in their old bedroom; the one they had shared before moving into the new house.

When Miranda awoke the next morning, she

looked out the window and shouted.

"Margot! Wake up. It's beautiful! Let's go out-side before we have to go to school."

They both dressed quickly and stepped out into a dazzling world of sparkling white snow and sunshine. After a visit to the chicken coop to feed and water Miranda's pets, they ran to their own house, almost bumping into Dad as he opened the back door.

"Good morning, girls! We missed you last night. The house is just way too quiet without you in it," he said, tossing a snowball at Miranda.

She laughed and grabbed a handful of snow to hurl back at him, and the fight was on. With squeals of laughter and shrieks of excitement, they pelted each other until Mom came to the door to call Miranda in.

"Where's Margot?" Miranda asked.

"She came in a long time ago and is already dressed for school. If you don't hurry you'll be late."

With a parting shot, she hit her dad square on the shoulder with a snowball and dove behind the door before he could get her back.

The phone was ringing as she entered the kitchen.

"Hello?" she said.

"Miranda? This is Colton. Higgins didn't get back from his nephews because of the storm so I'm doing all the chores. I heard Queen having a conniption fit, so I checked on her, and I can't find Shooting Star. She's not in the paddock."

 Chapter Seven

When Miranda arrived at Shady Hills with her father and Christopher Bergman, she ran to Starlight's stall. On the way over, they had decided they would saddle their horses and ride the pasture until they found the foal. Dad hurried off to consult with Colton and start searching on foot. Queen whinnied repeatedly, but they could hear no answering little neigh.

"It makes no sense!" Miranda exclaimed. "Why would she leave her mother?"

"And how?" Chris added. "I didn't think she could get out of the paddock."

"Too bad the snow covered everything, or we might've been able to follow her tracks," Miranda said. "Let's look for a hole in the fence before we start out. It might give us a clue."

Dad and Colton were already walking toward the far end of Queen's paddock. Exposed to the wind, the end away from the stable was swept clean of snow.

"Look!" Colton shouted. "The bottom rail is broken, leaving just enough room under the fence for a foal to scoot under, don't you think?"

"Only if she was lying down," Dad said. "She could have done that; lie down beside the fence, maybe roll over and stand up on the other side."

"Then the wind could have driven her away. It was blowing awfully hard last night," Colton said.

"Which way was it blowing?" Miranda asked.

"Out of the east, by the looks of the drifts," Dad said. "That would have pushed her along the fence toward the river."

Miranda and Chris rode slowly along the fence, looking for hoof prints and any other sign of the sorrel filly.

"I don't think she'd try to cross the river. Why don't you follow along the river, while I go up on that hill and see what I can see from there?" Miranda suggested.

The trail up the hill toward the cave was slick with snow, but both Miranda and Starlight had been there before in the winter and it posed no real problem. Miranda dismounted in front of the cave and left Starlight "ground tied." It was one of the things she had taught him. When the reins were dropped on the ground, Starlight knew he was supposed to stand and wait. He nearly always did. Miranda climbed the rocky formation above the cave where she could stand and see for miles in almost every direction.

The view from the top of the formation was

breathtaking. The river, like a wide silver ribbon, glittered in the sun as it wound its way through the pasture. The distant hills were white with snow, and the leaves of the cottonwood and aspen were golden among the variegated greens of the firs, pines and junipers. She saw Christopher on Queen as they made their way along the river. Colton's dog was a mere black speck as he trotted behind them. She saw no other living thing. Parts of the landscape were swept by the wind, leaving waves of golden brown grass and gray rock in the snowy landscape.

Miranda stood enthralled, forgetting for a moment the seriousness of the mission she was on, when a very loud mournful howl pierced the stillness. It gave her goose bumps and she was immediately alert. The howl came again, this time in a duet, followed by a chorus of high-pitched yips. The sounds repeated in the same order and then fell silent. *Coyotes,* Miranda thought. *Sounds like dozens of them; at least a good-sized pack.* She knew, however, that a few could sound like many.

She scanned the landscape in the direction the sound had come from, but saw nothing. She turned to look at Chris. Queen was standing still. Maybe Chris had heard it, too. Looking back again, Miranda saw two whitetail deer walking slowly across a meadow, stopping frequently to look back toward a rocky ravine. Their tails stood straight in the air and wagged like white flags every few seconds. Then they continued on, stopped, and looked back.

A very large coyote emerged from the ravine and

trotted slowly, nose to the ground, away from the deer. Three slightly smaller coyotes appeared at intervals. Each took a different path and meandered about looking for breakfast, Miranda supposed. She turned her attention to the big one and saw him dart after a rabbit. The rabbit disappeared in a rock pile, and the coyote trotted on in Miranda's direction. He disappeared into a thicket of wild rose bushes, leafless now, but tall and thick enough to hide him.

She saw two more deer come out of the far side of the thicket. They stopped and stomped their feet with their tails in the air. Their back legs were spread, and they seemed to be crouching, ready to run. They faced opposite directions, one watching one of the smaller coyotes and the other facing the rose thicket. Suddenly a terrified whinny broke the stillness, and Shooting Star streaked from the thicket toward the two deer. They bolted and bounded away. The large coyote was running after Shooting Star!

Miranda screamed.

"Chris! Quick, help her," she hollered, but he was too far away to hear and in a shallow gully which kept him from seeing the fleeing foal.

Miranda jumped down from the rock she was standing on and half ran, half slid down the hill to Starlight. Startled, he shied away and began trotting down the hill.

"Starlight, wait!" she called.

He slowed, but kept going. She whistled. It was a call she had taught him to come to. When he heard it, he stopped, turned, and trotted back to her. She got on

quickly and urged him down the hill, around the rock formation, toward the meadow where she had last seen Shooting Star. As soon as she could safely do so, she let Starlight run. He leaped forward and quickly gained on the coyote. Before they reached it, the coyote nipped at Shooting Star's heels and pulled her down. She struggled up quickly, veering sideways, but the coyote jumped at her again.

In the next instant Starlight was upon them, knocking the coyote down as he ran over it. Starlight skidded to a stop, while Miranda held on with both hands to keep from going over the saddle horn. Spinning around, Starlight struck the coyote with his front hooves, then reached down, grabbed it with his teeth and shook it. When he finally dropped it, the coyote lay limp on the ground. A frantic whinny reached Miranda's ear and she turned to see Chris on Queen racing toward them. Shooting Star squealed and ran to meet them.

As Lucky bounded toward her, tail wagging, Miranda dismounted to examine the limp body of the coyote. It was a very large male with a thick coat of fur. Lucky's hackles rose and a low growl escaped from deep inside him as he sniffed the carcass.

"What happened?" Chris asked, as he dismounted.

Shooting Star began to nurse the moment her mother stopped moving. Miranda told Chris all she had seen from the moment she heard the coyotes.

"I thought they only came out and hunted at night," Chris said.

"I sort of thought that too, but apparently not," Miranda said. "Maybe the storm kept them in their den all night. It's a good thing, or Shooting Star might have been their supper."

"What should we do with the carcass?" Chris asked.

"I think there's a bounty on them, and we could sell the hide," Miranda said, "but I don't want to bother with it now. We can tell Dad or Mr. Taylor and they might want to come get it."

Chris, Laurie, Miranda, and Margot gathered around the big dining-room table with poster board from Bergman's store. They had some markers, rulers and stencils that Laurie had brought. Chris and Miranda hadn't gone to school the day Shooting Star got lost, and her evening had been filled with homework to make up for the classes missed. But today her friends had rallied to help put their plan into action.

LOCAL STALLION CHALLENGES DERBY WINNERS TO SAVE DOOMED HORSE

A special horse, Sea Foam, is in danger.
Help Starlight save her by making a pledge.

STARLIGHT, of Shady Hills Horse Ranch,
will run against the average time (2 Min. 4/5 Sec.)
of the last 10 Kentucky Derby winners.

Please pledge $10 or more for every 1/5 second that
Starlight beats this time.
The money will help us buy Sea Foam and save her
from slaughter.
You can watch Starlight run at
Shady Hills Racetrack
Saturday, October 22, at 2 p.m.

"I'm surprised Mr. Taylor is letting you have all the money since he has half interest in Starlight, and especially since it's his track," Laurie said.

"Yeah. I never know what to expect from him," Miranda said. "Maybe he wants to show Starlight off to everyone. He knows how fast he is; even faster when I ride him than when Colton does."

Miranda, Margot, Chris, and Laurie put their signs up all over the school building and throughout town the next day. They went to every house and store in town asking for pledges.

"I'm not going to my Dad's store," Chris said. "I'm not about to ask him for money!"

"Okay. I'll take your store. Wish me luck," Miranda said, heading into Bergman's General Store.

"You've got to be kidding me," said Mr. Bergman, when Miranda handed him the flyer. "Who's going to ride him?"

"I am."

"Do you pay me for every fifth of a second he goes over the real race horses' time?"

"Over? No. If we don't go faster than the Kentucky Derby average we posted, you don't have to pay anything, that's all."

"Well, at least I have nothing to lose. I could bet a hundred and not be out anything, but put me down for twenty bucks for every fifth of a second less than the derby winners' time. If I get around to it, I'll come watch, as long as you promise not to cry when you lose," Mr. Bergman said with a chuckle.

Miranda didn't smile as she wrote down his pledge and asked him to sign it. By the end of the day, she was in a very bad mood. She had received a similar response from almost everyone she talked to. The upside to everyone's low expectations was that they pledged a lot of money just to prove that they didn't think Miranda stood a chance of winning. When they tallied all the pledges, they had four hundred fifty dollars for every fifth of a second faster than the Kentucky Derby time.

The weather cleared by the following Saturday, a week before Starlight's race against the clock. The snow was gone and the sun was bright.

"See, Margot?" Miranda said, knowing Margot feared the weather would interfere with their only hope of rescuing Sea Foam. "If it's like this next Saturday, there'll be no problem for the race."

The phone rang.

"Can you come stay with Elliot today? I have to go to Bozeman for a while," Mr. Taylor said when Miranda answered.

"Sure, I think so. Let me ask."

Mom agreed and said she'd drive her over.

"May I bring Margot along?" Miranda asked Mr. Taylor.

"Sure, as long as you keep an eye on both of them and don't get into any mischief yourself."

"Where's Colton?" Miranda asked.

"On his way to Kansas. He got a call from his folks yesterday. His grandmother passed away and he wanted to get there in time for the funeral. Took that clunky old car of his and his unlucky dog! I'll be lucky if they make it back in one piece!" Mr. Taylor grumbled.

It was too bad about Colton's grandma, but good for Miranda that he was away. She hadn't had much chance to baby-sit since he came to Shady Hills. He lived right there and was older, so Miranda became the second choice when Mr. Taylor needed a sitter.

"Let's play in the old barn," Elliot suggested as Mr. Taylor drove away.

"I get to swing on the rope first," Margot said.

Miranda agreed, and they all went to the hayloft. Pretending they were trapeze artists in a circus, each one tried to outdo the other in the tricks they performed, as they swung on the thick rope that hung from the peak of the roof. Hanging from a pulley attached to a metal beam, the rope had been used for lifting hay into the barn in the old days. Now it made a perfect swing. When they tired of that game, they played hide-and-seek until Miranda was hungry.

"Let's go in the house and fix sandwiches," Miranda said, when she finally found both Margot and Elliot in their separate hiding places.

"We can play checkers while we eat," Elliot suggested. "Oh, I guess we should think of a game we can all play," he added.

"If Higgins came over from the bunkhouse and brought his board we could all play," Miranda said. "Want to go ask him?"

"Oh, he isn't here. He's visiting his nephew," Elliot said.

"That's okay. We'll eat first, then you and Margot can play checkers while I make you some dessert."

Grandma had taught Miranda a simple fudge recipe years before. The only trick was to cook it for exactly the right length of time, which could be determined by dropping a little into cold water to see if it formed a soft ball. If it cooked too long and the ball was too hard, the fudge would be hard and sugary. If you didn't cook it long enough it would be sticky and never set up. Miranda was determined to watch it carefully and test it often, to get it just right. After finding all the ingredients she needed in Mr. Taylor's cupboard, she began mixing them together as Margot and Elliot began their game of checkers.

Miranda soon had the mixture bubbling and stood over it with a spoon and a cup of cold water, ready to begin the testing. A sudden roar broke the peaceful quiet and shook the kitchen.

"Why is that plane flying so low?" Elliot asked, jumping up from the table.

Chapter Eight

Miranda rushed to the kitchen door as the sound of another plane rattled the kitchen window. Margot crowded past her, and they all ran into the yard and looked up. Two more planes roared in the sky, so close to the ground that Miranda could see the pilots through the window.

"Those aren't little planes!" she exclaimed.

"They look like fighter jets," Elliot said. "Are they going to bomb us?"

"Don't be silly. Maybe they're getting ready for an air show or something," Miranda said.

As the four planes disappeared over the hills, the children turned to go back into the house. The sound of pounding hooves stopped them.

"It sure scared the horses," Elliot said. "Look at them go!"

A dozen two-year-old fillies thundered toward

the far end of the field below the barn.

"Let's check on our horses," Miranda said, running toward the stable.

Starlight was running down his paddock, snorting and stomping. He wheeled when he reached the end and galloped back toward them. Queen and Shooting Star were nervous but seemed to be okay. Lady stood as still as a statue, staring at the horizon where the planes had disappeared.

"Sunny is shut up in her stall. I wanted her to be ready in case we wanted to ride," Elliot said, running to check on his horse.

Miranda was right behind him when he unlatched the door. The frightened mare shoved against the door as soon as it began to open, knocking Elliot down as she broke for freedom. Miranda helped him up.

"I'm okay," he said, running after his horse.

Sunny ran down the driveway in front of the stables, gradually slowed down and stopped to nibble some sprigs of grass along the fence of the round pen.

"Get the halter and I'll help you catch her," Miranda said to Elliot.

Sunny lifted her head and trotted away when she saw Miranda approaching with a halter in hand. Elliot ran to head her off.

"Open the door to the arena," Miranda called. "Maybe we can get her in there."

But Sunny turned and bolted back past Miranda, head down, tail flying. She trotted down the lane past the old barn and stopped at the fence of the field where the fillies grazed.

"She wants to play games," Miranda said. "Maybe if I got on Starlight . . ."

"Eeeek! Miranda, the house is on fire!" Margot screamed.

Miranda turned to stare at dark gray smoke escaping from the kitchen door, which they had left open.

"Oh, no. My fudge!"

Miranda ran to the house, clasped her hand over

her nose, and plunged in. Through the haze that burned her eyes, she saw that all the smoke came from the pan on the stove. She snatched it by the handle, anxious to get away from the choking smoke.

"Owww!" she screamed, dropping the pan on the floor.

Choking and sobbing, she held her right wrist with her left hand and bent to the floor.

"Get out of there!" Mr. Taylor's voice boomed.

A hand on her arm pulled her to her feet and propelled her toward the door. Mr. Taylor came out behind her, holding the smoking pan in his gloved hand. He dropped it in the trash can.

"Oh Mr. Taylor, I'm so sorry," Miranda said sobbing. "I wanted to do everything perfect. I completely forgot about the fudge until I saw the smoke."

"You could have burned the house down!" Mr. Taylor yelled. "Stay right where you are, all three of you, while I get some windows open and some fans turned on."

"Let me, Mr. Taylor," Miranda begged. "It's my fault and that smoke is awful. You shouldn't . . ."

But Mr. Taylor was gone and there was nothing to do but wait as he had ordered. If he didn't come out soon, Miranda decided, she'd go in looking for him. She was about to do it when he came out, coughing and wiping his eyes.

"Are you okay, Mr. Taylor?" Miranda asked. When he nodded, she continued, "I'm very sorry. I will pay you back for the pan I ruined, I promise."

"Ha," Mr. Taylor said, with a laugh that sounded

more like a growl. "That pan is the least of my worries. I'll probably have to replace all the curtains, drapes, bedding and half the furniture. I thought you'd grown up enough for me to count on you, but I come home to see my house engulfed in smoke! I should have known you'd do something to cost me more money. You always do. Now go to the tack shed and call your grandma to come get you."

"It was an accident, Grandfather," Miranda heard Elliot say, as she hurried to get away from the old man's wrath.

Tears streamed down her face, so that she could hardly see to dial. Her heart ached, and her hand stung so badly she could hardly bear it.

"Please come get Margot and me," she said, trying to make her voice sound ordinary.

She knew she'd failed when Grandma asked, "What's wrong? Are you okay?"

"We're okay. I'll tell you about it when you get here."

She hung up the phone and ran to Starlight's stall. She threw her arms around his neck and then stepped back, wincing with pain. She expected to see flames coming from her hand when she looked down at it, but her palm was just very red. She stuck it into Starlight's water trough and the pain subsided.

Grandma insisted on stopping at the clinic, but it wasn't open on Saturdays. She called the emergency number posted on the door. The nurse on call came almost immediately.

"That's a nasty burn. See, it's starting to blister already. The best thing you can do is to protect it from infection. I am going to put an ointment on it and bandage it," she said as she worked, "but, not too tightly. Now, don't get it wet and don't break the blister." Turning towards Grandma, she added, "Give her ibuprofen every four hours for pain as needed, and she'll need it to sleep tonight. Call us if you need stronger pain medicine and I'll get the doctor to call in a prescription."

It was several miles to any drug store, so Miranda figured she'd just have to endure the pain.

"Let's hope Colton gets back in time to ride Starlight for you next Saturday," Dad said when he kissed Miranda good night. "You'll have to postpone your race if he's not."

"Why, Dad?" Miranda asked in alarm. "You said I could ride."

"That was before you burned your hand. You heard what the nurse said about not breaking that blister. We can't take chances and have you get a bad infection."

Miranda didn't sleep much that night, for every time she dozed off and bumped it, even on her pillow or blankets, she cried out in pain. When she could stand it no longer, she went to the kitchen, put ice in a pan of water, and plunged her hand into it. Taking it to the living room she sat on the couch, one hand in ice water, the other holding a book.

"You're up bright and early. How is your hand this morning?" Dad asked as he came out of the bedroom, fully dressed and ready to go to work. "Hey! Didn't the nurse tell you not to put it in water?"

"But it feels better if I keep it cold," Miranda replied.

"If it hurts that much Mom can take you to the emergency room in Bozeman to get a doctor to look at it this morning," Dad said. "That's a bad burn and will be a lot worse if it gets infected."

"Da-ad," Miranda wailed. "It'll be okay. I have to go to Shady Hills today. It's Sunday, and everyone will be there."

"Oh, no! That's just asking for trouble. You would try to do everything you always do. If you break that blister and get dirt in it, who knows how long it'll take to heal? You might even have to have skin grafts. It's worse than you want to admit, and that's why I want a doctor to look at it."

"Please let me go, Dad," Miranda begged, her voice breaking as tears filled her eyes. "I have to talk to Mr. Taylor. That's all I could think about when I couldn't sleep last night. He was so angry. I nearly destroyed his house and I want to see what I can do to make it up to him. I hate having him mad at me, especially when I know I deserve it."

"Oh," Dad said gently as he dried and rewrapped Miranda's hand. "I didn't realize what you were going through. I'm sure Mr. Taylor isn't mad at you. After all, it was an accident."

"Please let me go talk to him. I don't want to do it over the phone."

"Maybe if you're very careful that it doesn't get

bumped or wet, it can wait until tomorrow when Doctor Davis is in her office," Dad conceded, referring to Miranda's pediatrician. "But you must promise to keep it wrapped and out of harm's way."

"Thank you, Dad!"

"But wait. Let me hear you promise you won't be trying to ride, or longe, or even brush or halter Starlight," Dad said.

"I promise."

Dad dropped Miranda off at the big ranch house before continuing on to the hay barn, where he parked and began morning chores. He still worked for Mr. Taylor part time and had been coming every day since Colton left.

Miranda knocked timidly on the kitchen door, carefully holding her right hand next to her chest. Mr. Taylor opened the door almost immediately. Looking into his frowning face, Miranda was tempted to turn and leave.

"What do you want?"

To Miranda, the question sounded more like a growl.

"I want to apologize for what I did to your house yesterday," she said, standing her ground. "I want to see what I can do to pay for the damages."

"Come in," Mr. Taylor said, as he stood aside and opened the door wider.

"I'm really sorry. I was irresponsible. But I didn't mean to, and it will never happen again," Miranda said, trying to keep from crying.

"Sit down, Miranda. I know it was an accident. I'm not angry," Mr. Taylor said. "I just can't convince you that I'm not a mean old ogre, can I?"

"You were so mad at me yesterday, I didn't think you'd ever forgive me."

"I may have seemed angry, but that's just how I come across when I'm scared or upset. Elliot told me all about the airplanes scaring the horses. It's no wonder you forgot. Darned planes shouldn't have been anywhere near here!"

"What were they doing?"

"I heard it was an Air Force training mission that flew off course."

"Oh. Well, anyway, I shouldn't have gone out and left the stove turned on. I'll make it up to you," Miranda said.

"Don't worry about it. There really wasn't much damage. I left the windows open all night, and most of the smell was gone this morning. I lost one old pan. That's about it."

"Really? But you said you'd have to replace the furniture and drapes and everything. I'll have more money than we need from the race next Saturday, and I'll give you all but the amount we need to buy Sea Foam."

"Miranda, are you listening? I don't need it. I will not have to replace my furniture," Mr. Taylor said. "How is your hand?"

"It has a pretty big blister and it hurts some," Miranda said, "but I think it'll be fine. It has to be by next weekend, because Dad won't let me ride Starlight in the race if it isn't."

"Let me get this clear. You actually got people to pledge money on a race against the clock?"

"Yes, it's almost like he's running in the Kentucky Derby, because he has to beat the average time of the last ten winners. Lots of people pledged money and they'll be here Saturday!"

"Well, I'll be! Now, there's some publicity for Shady Hills! Because if he wins on my little track, I'm taking him to the next Kentucky Derby. We might even go for the Triple Crown!" he exclaimed, laughing and slapping her on the back.

Oh, no. If I win, I lose Starlight again, Miranda thought.

As she walked to the stables, she met Higgins. He was on her list of people to ask for pledges. Though her heart wasn't in it, she asked him.

"Nah, I'm not much of a gambler, but even if I was, I wouldn't bet against a horse I was sure would win!" Higgins said.

Chapter Nine

Miranda was almost sick with worry over Mr. Taylor's comment. She should have seen that coming, but it took her by surprise. She knew from the research paper she had done last year that the Triple Crown comprised three grueling races, all of them far from Montana. She didn't dare hope that her parents would let her go with Mr. Taylor and Starlight, and she could hardly stand the thought of letting Starlight go without her.

"You sure are quiet tonight," Margot said to Miranda, as the two girls got ready for bed. "Is it because your hand hurts?"

"No. It's getting better. I'm just thinking about the race next Saturday."

"Then I'd think you'd be excited. You seem sad."

"Well, I don't know what's going to happen.

Colton isn't here, and Dad might not let me ride," Miranda said, leaving out her biggest worry.

"Oh, no! We can't call it off. They'll sell Sea Foam before I get a chance . . . ," Margot began.

"No they won't. I called again and talked to the lady. I wanted them to know what we were doing. She even pledged ten dollars. She said she wouldn't let anybody take Sea Foam to the auction."

"Then why are you so worried? We can just put it off a week until Colton gets back."

"I don't want Colton to ride. I want to. Besides, I have another problem now. Mr. Taylor is going to take Starlight to the Kentucky Derby if he wins."

"Wouldn't you like to have your horse win the Kentucky Derby?"

"It's not just the Derby. After that it's the Preakness and then the Belmont Stakes. Mr. Taylor wants to win the whole Triple Crown."

"What's that?"

"That's when a horse wins all three of those races. Only eleven horses have ever done it in the whole history of horse racing. The first one was in 1919. The problem is the Kentucky Derby is in the first part of May, before school is out. The last race isn't until June. Mom would never let me go."

"You wouldn't try to lose just to keep Mr. Taylor from taking him, would you?" Margot asked accusingly.

"Of course not!" Miranda exclaimed, though she had been thinking of that very thing. She didn't want to lose this chance to save Sea Foam, but maybe they'd find another way.

"Can just any horse enter? I thought they had to be from Kentucky."

"Margot! That's it. That's what I was forgetting. A horse can be from anywhere, not just from Kentucky, but it's only for three-year-olds. Starlight is too old to enter. There's no way Mr. Taylor can take him to those races!" Miranda jumped up and hugged Margot. "Ouch!" she yelled as she jumped back, shielding her throbbing hand.

Miranda slept better that night, only waking up a few times. She made an ice pack and held it against the bandage, though she wasn't sure she was supposed to.

"Let me see," Mom said when Miranda sat down to eat the next morning. "How does it feel?"

"It's much better, Mom. I don't think I need to see a doctor."

"Do you think you can go to school?"

"Sure. I'll have to try to write with my left hand, but at least I won't miss my classes."

Seventh grade was her hardest year yet, with a teacher who felt it was her duty to prepare her students not only for high school, but college as well. Miranda had homework every night even though she worked hard at school.

"All right, but come home after school," Mom said. "I don't want you messing with the horses until that hand is healed."

Miranda was bent over her homework at the dining room table that night when the phone rang.

"It's for you Miranda," Mom called. "It's Colton."

"Hi, Miranda. I just got in. Mr. Taylor told me about your hand. Are you okay?" asked Colton with concern.

"It's getting better. I think I'll be able to ride on Saturday," Miranda said hastily.

"Mr. Taylor said I might have to ride for you, but if you can, that's fine by me."

Miranda asked about his trip, offered sympathy that it had been a sad occasion, and told him she'd see him tomorrow. With a sigh, she went back to her homework. As much as she liked Colton, she had hoped he would stay away until after the race. Her parents were not likely to let her ride when having Colton take her place was an option. Her fears were confirmed the next morning when her mother told her to come home after school again.

"But Mom. My hand hardly hurts anymore. I haven't been able to do anything with Starlight since Friday. I was busy taking care of kids on Saturday, and on Sunday all I could do was say hi to him. Besides, I need to talk to Colton."

"Maybe it would be all right, if she promises not to ride, or even work Starlight from the ground," Dad suggested.

"Barry, it's hard enough to say no to this young lady without you taking her side," Mom complained, "but I give up! Do you promise to let Colton do all the work and keep your hand wrapped and out of harm's way?"

"I promise. But my hand really is almost healed.

I'm sure it'll be fine by Saturday."

"We'll see about that then," her father said.

Saturday dawned sunny, but cold. Miranda was so excited she could hardly stand it. No longer worried about Mr. Taylor's threat to take Starlight to the Kentucky Derby, she was eager to show the people of the community what he could do. Just to make sure that everyone who pledged money on the race would be there, she telephoned each of them, reminding them not to miss the afternoon race.

"I wouldn't think of it," Mr. Bergman and some of the others commented. "A little Country View schoolgirl who thinks she can beat the time of the fastest racehorses in the country? I'll have to see it to believe it. I'm bringing my stopwatch."

She finished phoning everyone by the time Dad came in from helping Grandpa with the milking. Mom came into the kitchen in her robe, looking sleepy and tousled. She was not a morning person.

"Miranda, don't you have breakfast ready?" Mom asked.

"I didn't realize it was so late. I was reminding people to come watch me race today," Miranda said cheerfully. "I have coffee made, though. I'll scramble some eggs and have them ready in a minute."

"I don't remember telling you that you could ride in the race today, Miranda," Mom said. "We told you that if Colton made it back, he would have to ride for you."

"But my hand is fine!" Miranda protested. "I have to ride. People are expecting me to. Do you want me to break my promise?"

"Miranda! I don't like to hear you take that tone with your mother. You had no right to tell people you would be riding after we told you that you couldn't," Dad said.

"You said I could ride if my hand was better! It is! Don't you two have any idea how important this is to me?"

Flooded with anger and disappointment, Miranda felt she had to flee. Slamming the door behind her, she ran from the house and crawled through the fence that divided the river pasture on the Caruthers' place from their backyard. She ran blindly, imagining her father coming after her, ready to bring her back and face her punishment. When she stopped running and looked back, no one was there.

Tears ran down Miranda's face, as she stooped beneath the low branches of an old willow tree, plopped to the ground and leaned against the trunk. Her anger subsided, as fear took its place. She hadn't acted like that since her dad had come home. What did he think of her, now? She knew her mother would ground her for such behavior. Did that mean she wouldn't be able to go to the race at all? She sobbed, wishing she could take back her angry words and actions. It was bad enough that they weren't going to let her ride, but she would die, she thought, if she couldn't go at all.

She didn't know how long she sat there crying, but she was surprised—and suddenly worried—that no one came looking for her. Remembering that she hadn't even done her chores that morning, she got up and hur-

ried home. She met Margot coming from the chicken house.

"I forgot to feed my chickens and rabbits," Miranda said. "Did you do it for me?"

Margot nodded.

"They're really mad at me, aren't they?" Miranda asked.

Again Margot nodded.

"Look, I'm sorry. Don't worry. The race will go on even if I'm not there, and Starlight will win," Miranda said. "You'll still get your Sea Foam."

"I know. I'm not worrying about that," Margot said softly. "I just want you to go. I want you to be able to ride because I know you want to, and you can ride him better than anyone, but I don't think they'll let you."

Miranda was afraid Margot was right.

"I'm sorry, Mom," Miranda said as she entered the kitchen. "I got so upset, I wasn't thinking straight. I know I shouldn't talk to you like that, and I didn't fix breakfast."

"Breakfast was not the problem, Miranda. Your temper is a problem. I should ground you for a week for disrespecting your parents like that."

"I know, Mom. But please don't. I really need to go, even if I can't ride. I want to be there to explain to people and at least watch," Miranda said. "If you have to ground me, please wait until after the race."

"You can go to the race. Barry and I talked it over, but I'm not about to let you ride, not after the way you talked to me!"

Miranda found Colton in Starlight's stall, already brushing Starlight's coat to an iridescent shine. Starlight greeted her with a low rumbling nicker and nosed her shirt pocket for a treat. Miranda smiled at Colton as they listened to Mr. Taylor joke with one of the biggest cattle ranchers in the area.

"I think he's glad to have an occasion to show off his ranch," Colton whispered to Miranda as they led

Starlight past Mr. Taylor who was cheerfully directing traffic.

By two o'clock, a large crowd gathered around the fence that surrounded the oval track. Miranda stood with Colton and Starlight behind the starting gate. Standing on a platform nearby, Mr. Taylor picked up a microphone and greeted the crowd.

"I didn't know he had a P. A. system," Miranda said in surprise.

"He spent two days getting that set up," Colton said. "He's making the most of this."

"As my track is exactly half the size of the Kentucky Derby track, Starlight will circle it twice," Mr. Taylor said. "Mind you, that's a disadvantage to the horse and advantage to all of you who are betting against him. He has more turns and shorter straightaways."

"I wish the crowd would back away from the fence a bit," Colton complained. "It's going to distract Starlight; make him nervous."

"Just talk to him, like you always do; give him his head, and don't fight him," Miranda advised.

"Oh, no!" Colton said. "Here comes my dog. I should've . . ."

But Margot was already on the track calling Lucky. The dog turned and ran toward her, wagging his tail.

"Put him in the tack shed, Mar," Miranda shouted. "And thanks!"

Starlight pranced and tossed his head when Miranda led him into the starting gate. He knew what was in store and was eager to run. As soon as the gate opened he sprang into action. Then he slowed, looking from side to side as if to say, "Hey, where are the other horses?" Colton leaned over his neck and Miranda knew he was trying to get Starlight to focus on the race, not on the bystanders. Starlight slowed a little more as he looked at the crowd, but soon he was past them and he surged forward at Colton's bidding. Miranda stood between Mr. Taylor and her father, watching breathlessly as Starlight seemed to fly past her. Again, he slowed slightly as he looked at the crowd, but made up for it as soon as they were behind him.

"Why aren't you riding?" Chris asked, climbing the fence beside her.

"Mom wouldn't let me."

"People are gonna be disappointed!"

"How do you think I feel? Just watch!" Miranda exclaimed, irritated at the interruption.

As Starlight swept across the finish line, Mr. Taylor snapped his stopwatch.

"Two minutes and two-fifths of a second!" he shouted, laughing and slapping Mr. Bergman on the back. "I told you I had the fastest horse in the country. That's two-fifths of a second better than the average time of the past ten Kentucky Derby winners. Pay the young lady here, everyone. Two times your pledge!"

"No way!" shouted Mr. Bergman. "Why wasn't Miranda on that horse? This whole thing has been misrepresented, and I'm not paying a cent until I see Miranda ride. She said *she* could beat the Derby winners, not some professional jockey. What are you people trying to pull?"

Miranda felt her face burn as several other men in the group joined in agreement with Bergman.

"Miranda has a third-degree burn on her hand. She wanted to ride, but I wouldn't let her," Mom said, yelling above the other voices.

"Whatever your excuse, the deal is off if she doesn't ride herself," said one of the disgruntled men.

"Do you mean to say that you think Starlight would have lost if Miranda had been riding?" Dad asked the men.

"No one would expect a child to get the same results as a professional," Mr. Bergman said. "I wouldn't have pledged a cent if I hadn't been told that Miranda would be riding. We came to see her make good on her promise, not to watch a professional rider. We could stay home and see that on TV."

"Miranda, do you think you can ride without hurting your hand?" Mom asked.

"Sure I can, Mom. I don't even have to use it, and I have it wrapped so it won't get bumped. It hardly hurts anymore."

"Then get on and show these guys what you can do!" Mom exclaimed.

"Maybe we should let Starlight cool down for a few minutes," Dad said.

"I've got work to do. I can't stand around here all day waiting," Mr. Smythe complained. Several others, including Mr. Bergman agreed.

"It's okay, Dad. He can do it without a rest. He isn't even sweating."

Colton adjusted the stirrups for Miranda and helped her on.

"Her helmet! We didn't bring it because we didn't plan for her to ride," Mom exclaimed. "Can she wear yours, Colton?"

Colton took it off and handed it to her as he held Starlight, who was already prancing in excitement.

"Get down, Miranda. I'll help you put that on and make sure it's buckled securely. This doesn't mean I'm forgetting how you behaved," Mom added as she helped Miranda back into the saddle. "Now don't get hurt, or I'll hate myself for changing my mind."

Chapter Ten

When the starting gate opened, Miranda couldn't help grabbing leather to keep her balance as Starlight surged into a full gallop. A sharp pain reminded her to keep her sore hand protected as she leaned forward, her face in his flowing mane.

"Good boy! Keep it up, Starlight. Show these people what you can really do. Don't pay a bit of attention to them; just run for me."

She felt another surge of speed as he lengthened his stride. His pounding hooves ate up the wet ground, and chunks of mud flew into the air, some hitting her back. She feared she might have been too hasty in prodding him into running full out. She eased back into the saddle, but Starlight didn't slow down. As he sped past the crowd again, Miranda saw only a blur in her peripheral vision. People shouted. Starlight lowered his head and ran even faster. Sure that he had never gone this fast before, Miranda crouched over his neck and shouted with pure joy.

"Thank you, Starlight. You are the best horse ever."

When she heard the roar of the crowd, she knew she was past the finish line. They had done it. They had not only beaten the Derby time, but the time Colton had made only a few minutes before. She knew it without being told. She sat back in the saddle, careful not to bump her hand again, and pulled back slightly on the reins.

"It's okay, boy. You can stop now. We have way more than enough to pay for Sea Foam. Whoa, Starlight," she said, as he began to slow and finally stopped in front of Mr. Taylor after circling the track again.

"This is incredible! I've never seen any horse run this fast! One minute, fifty nine and two-fifths seconds," Mr. Taylor told her. "Do you realize that's faster than any horse since . . ."

"Since Secretariat!" Miranda shouted. "He was the first horse to ever break two minutes! He ran the Kentucky Derby in a minute, fifty-nine and two-fifths seconds!" Miranda exclaimed excitedly.

"Now you all owe seven times your pledge," Dad said, as he beamed at Miranda.

"I knew you could do it," Higgins said, coming out of the crowd to congratulate her.

"It's because she's so light. If it was a real race she'd have to have weight added," began Mr. Bergman.

Higgins put his hand on Mr. Bergman's arm. "I heard you insist Miranda ride, but I don't recall you asking for a handicap."

"I know. I plan to pay. I was just saying . . ."

"He's right, you know, Miranda." Mr. Taylor said. "When we practice for the big races, we'll have to add some weight to his saddle."

"Big races?" Miranda protested. "But he's too old to enter the Derby!"

"Oh, I know that. I was just kidding about the Derby, but there are other races with big purses."

What had she done? Even if Starlight couldn't race in the Kentucky Derby, she should have known that Mr. Taylor would want him back on the racing tour after a showing like this.

When the Shady Hills pickup arrived at the dude ranch outside of Anaconda, Miranda and Margot jumped out and ran to the corrals. They had phoned ahead to say they would be coming to pick up Sea Foam. Dad drove the truck, pulling the two-horse trailer behind it. A woman came out of the house and called to them.

"You must be Miranda and Margot," she said with a smile, extending her hand. "I'm Patty Coleway, and I talked to you on the phone. Chalky's in the corral over here."

Patty's brown ponytail bounced against the back of her neck as she led the way. She wasn't much taller than Miranda and wore faded blue jeans, with a pair of leather gloves stuffed into a back pocket. Her cowboy boots were scuffed and dirty. She turned and smiled at them as she opened the gate. Her white teeth flashed in contrast to her suntanned face.

"I can't tell you how glad I am that you're buying Chalky. I love this little horse. I raised her on a bottle after her mother died of complications giving birth. When my father saw that she had a malformed hip, he wanted to have her put down. That was five years ago. I've been fighting for her life ever since."

"You mean she's only five years old?" Miranda asked.

"She looks older, doesn't she? That's because of her limp and the fact that she didn't get a good start on her mother's milk, I think. Her color doesn't help much either. But she was born that way. Her mother was a palomino, and she got enough of that to look like a yellow-stained, white-headed old woman. But she is much healthier than she looks. Ought to be good for many more years."

"She's very gentle and well trained for five," Miranda commented as she watched Margot walk up to Sea Foam and pet her face.

"I trained her myself. She was such a pet, she followed me everywhere. Since she was so easy to handle, I convinced my dad that she was worth her keep by using her for a kid's horse on the trail rides. But when we went through a business slump last summer, all the men here, including my husband and my father, ganged up on me. They said we couldn't keep any but the best horses. If you hadn't promised to buy her, she would have gone to the auction and probably the slaughterhouse," Patty said. "I'm so grateful you took pity on her."

"It's not pity. It's love," Miranda said. "I know how Margot feels about her!"

"Well, we'd better get her loaded, I guess," Patty said gruffly, brushing away a tear. "Did you bring a halter?"

Dad, who had walked up behind them, handed a bright blue halter to Miranda. The girls had picked it out at Bergman's General Store after yesterday's race. They would wait until they could go to Bozeman or Butte to get a saddle, saddle pad, bridle and helmet for Margot, for Bergman's General Store carried only a limited supply of farm and ranch equipment.

Miranda put the halter on the little horse and led her out of the corral to the trailer, which Dad had backed up near the gate. When Sea Foam saw the small confines of the trailer, she balked and backed up. Miranda patted her and talked to her and then tried again. Sea Foam fought the rope, shaking her head. When Dad put his hand on her rump, she backed up even faster, almost sitting down.

"Maybe you should lead her in," Miranda said, handing the lead rope to Patty. "She knows and trusts you."

But Patty had no better success.

"She's never been loaded into a trailer before. I haven't ever taken her anywhere, and I never even thought about training her to load. I think she's scared to walk into the dark," Patty said. "Maybe if you open the feed doors to let light in, she won't be so nervous."

Dad opened the feed doors at the front of the trailer, but Sea Foam still balked. Two men approached

from the barn. Miranda recognized them as the wranglers who got them the horses they'd ridden with Mom and Grandma on the trail ride.

"Here, let us get her in for you," one of them said.

The other was carrying a lariat, which he tied to one side of the back of the trailer. He looped it behind Sea Foam and slipped it around a bar on the other side of the trailer. As the first man took the lead rope from Patty and walked into the trailer, the second man pulled the rope tight behind Sea Foam's rear end and, letting it slide through the bar, leaned on the rope with all his strength, forcing her forward. The first man had wrapped her lead rope around the center divider and was trying to lever her in with brute force. Sea Foam went wild, fighting the force by shaking her head back and forth and bracing herself with all four feet. Her head hit the inside of the trailer with a loud bang, and blood spurted from a gash just above her eye.

"Stop it!" Miranda screamed. "Quit! You're hurting her."

The men took no notice of her as they cursed the horse and applied more pressure.

Dad put his hand on one man's shoulder.

"Quit!" he shouted. "Now get away from my daughters' horse and go back where you came from."

When the men released the pressure they had on Sea Foam, she fell back so abruptly that she lost her footing, and fell on her haunches. She jumped up and stood trembling, her eyes wild with fear.

"Just trying to help," one of the wranglers said. "If you think you can do any better, be my guest. Just get her out of here, even if you have to tie her to the back and drag her home. If you don't, we'll get rid of her in our own way."

Patty stood at Sea Foam's head, trying to calm her, as Margot and Miranda approached slowly, patting her gently and talking in low tones.

"I am so sorry. I should have known it was bad news when those two offered to help. I just didn't know how we were going to get her loaded and I thought their way might work," Patty said. "This cut isn't very deep. I'll go get some water and disinfectant for it."

Miranda and Margot led Sea Foam around, talking softly to her and letting her eat grass when she finally calmed down. Margot went to the trailer and got some oat pellets to give to Sea Foam after her wound was treated. The horse ate the treat eagerly and followed Margot around the yard. The lead rope wasn't needed. Miranda saw the two men walking from the barn toward them. She felt anger boiling in her chest and started to go meet them. Her father strode past her toward the men. They turned around and went back into the barn.

"I was just going to see if they wanted to talk to us," Dad said, smiling at Miranda. "I guess not."

The men stayed out of sight after that.

Miranda went to Margot and Sea Foam, who were staying far from the trailer.

"She sure likes you," Miranda said.

"I love her!" Margot proclaimed, "but how are we going to get her home if we can't get her in the trailer?"

"Don't worry. We'll get her in. We just have to get it so it isn't so scary. Dad's taking out the center divider and using it for a ramp. It's made of solid wood, so she can walk up gradually," Miranda explained. "She's learning to trust you, so she might just follow you in."

Margot led Sea Foam back toward the trailer, but the little horse stopped, looked at the trailer nervously and backed up.

"Let me try something," Miranda said, taking the lead rope from Margot.

She led the little horse around until she got her circling at the end of the long halter rope. Patty, who had disappeared into the house after treating Sea Foam's cut, had evidently trained the little horse to longe.

"Let's see how well she backs," Miranda said. "Back, Girl."

Without any prodding, Sea Foam backed in a straight line.

"Good girl. That deserves a treat!" Miranda said, and Margot gave her horse another pellet.

"Back!" Miranda said again, and Sea Foam backed.

Miranda guided her backward, occasionally putting slight pressure on the halter to turn her. Miranda stopped to reward her with another oat pellet, but Sea Foam seemed perfectly happy to walk backward all day. Maybe it was a more comfortable action for her deformed hip, but whatever it was, Miranda decided to take advantage of it. She backed her in a big circle, talking to her the whole time and occasionally giving her treats to keep her attention. When Sea Foam backed up the slight incline of the ramp into the trailer, she didn't even seem to notice.

Miranda patted her, and Margot gave her still more treats as Dad shut the back gate of the trailer behind them. There was still plenty of light coming in over the back doors, and without the divider, the inside was as roomy as a small stall. Sea Foam showed no sign of fear, but sighed with contentment as the girls petted and fed her. When Dad opened one of the doors to slide the divider in against the far wall and fasten it so it couldn't fall over, Sea Foam showed no sign of alarm and made no effort to escape.

Patty came from the house as the girls climbed into the pickup.

"You got her loaded, and without hurting her, too!" she exclaimed. "I'm sorry I didn't help. I was so afraid you wouldn't be able to get her in, I just, well, I started crying, to tell the truth, and I had to be by myself for a while. I watched out the window when you backed her in. Now I know she'll have the best possible home, and it's not so hard to say good-bye. Maybe I can come see her sometime."

Dad drove very slowly out of the driveway. When he stopped at the road, Miranda jumped out to check on Sea Foam. She had lain down and didn't seem to be at all frightened. They stopped to check on her three more times on the way home. She was relaxed and seemed to be enjoying the ride.

It was nearly dark when they arrived home. After leading Sea Foam into the old barn for the night, they gave her fresh water and hay. The next day, after Margot brushed her and led her around for a while, they put her in a small pasture with the milk cows. Sea Foam seemed happy with her new surroundings. She even touched noses with one of the cows, as if to say, "Glad to meet you. I'm going to be staying with you, so we might as well be friends."

Miranda and Margot rode the school bus to the Shady Hills gate with Elliot the next day. Neither Chris nor Laurie was able to come, and Dad was already there helping Higgins sort a herd of yearlings, deciding which ones should be sold at Shady Hills' annual auction. Colton waited for them at the school bus stop so they wouldn't have to walk, for the weather had turned quite cold. The three kids crowded into Colton's little car as Lucky, tail wagging, tried to lick each one of them. On the way to the stables, Miranda told Colton all about Margot's new horse.

"We have money left over and we're saving it for the auction sale at the Caruthers' place next week. We hope we can buy some of his tack," Miranda said.

"I wish you would bring Sea Foam over here so we could ride together," Elliot said to Margot.

"It would be fun if all the horses were together," Margot said, "but Barry says we have all that free pasture, including the Caruthers' place he just bought. It would be silly to pay to board her over here."

"I've been thinking about taking Starlight home to our place, so Sea Foam will have company, and so I can ride with Margot," Miranda said.

"Uh, Miranda," Colton said, "I'd be surprised if Mr. Taylor would let you. He's going to Texas, and he wants to take Starlight."

Chapter Eleven

Miranda hurried to Mr. Taylor's house when Colton pulled into his usual parking place beside the garage. She was trembling when Mr. Taylor opened the door to her knock.

"What are you planning? Were you just going to take Starlight to Texas without even talking to me?" Miranda demanded, a catch in her throat accompanying the angry tears she tried to blink back.

"Whoa, hold on there!" Mr. Taylor exclaimed. "I wasn't going to do anything with Starlight without telling you. Are you forgetting that he's still half mine, and that I have the controlling half until I die?"

"But when you found out you couldn't count on him to always father black foals, you wanted to geld him. You gave up on him. Then I thought you'd let me take him to my place any time I wanted to. It would be less expense for you."

"Miranda, when I found out he can run faster than any horse in the country, it doesn't matter what kind of foals he throws. He is worth his weight in gold just for the amount of money he can make on the race circuit."

"But you don't really need the money. Can't you wait until school's out so I can go with you?"

"You don't know a thing about my finances. I have to make a trip to Texas on other business. I'm taking Colton with me."

"But why? How long will you be gone?"

"I don't know," Mr. Taylor said soberly, sitting down at the kitchen table. "I just got a letter this morning. It had some bad news."

Miranda sat across from him and looked at the envelope in his hand. It was registered, and had the return address of a law office in Houston.

"My parents died, both of them, just two days apart, in a nursing home," he said sadly. "I haven't spoken to them for so long, I didn't even know they weren't still on the ranch. I am the only heir, and I have to go down and settle the estate. I may have to sell the ranch before I come back."

"Mr. Taylor, please don't take Starlight with you. It might take a long time! I can't stand to be away from him," Miranda begged.

"I guess you won't know what you can stand until you have to. That's life, Miranda. That's how it is for everybody. The sooner you learn it, the better off you'll be."

Two days later, Starlight was gone. Slumping into

the corner of his empty stall, Miranda sobbed uncontrollably. Her chest hurt so bad, she was sure her heart had actually broken. Though she had spent every moment with Starlight after hearing Mr. Taylor's awful news, she had not had enough time to properly tell her horse good-bye, and now he was gone. She was sure she would die of heartache before he returned.

Elliot was staying with his best friend, Mark Wagner, while Mr. Taylor was in Texas. Margot was at home with Sea Foam. Chris and Laurie had come with her to Shady Hills after school, but in her grief, Miranda was unaware of anyone else around her.

"Miranda," Laurie said gently, putting her arm around her friend's shoulder. "I'm sorry you're so sad. I didn't want to bother you, but you've been crying for an hour, and I got worried. Chris is, too. He wanted me to see if you would come help us with Shooting Star. He put her new halter on her, but we don't know how to get her to lead. She's really fighting it."

Miranda wiped her tears on her jacket sleeve. She had already used all the tissues she had found in her pockets. Her face was a mess and she knew it. One hour! It was hard to believe that much time had passed. On the other hand it seemed like an eternity. She wanted the ache in her chest to end. Choking back more tears, she got to her feet and followed Laurie to Queen's paddock, where Chris was standing in front of Shooting Star, scratching her neck. When he saw Miranda, he tugged on the lead rope.

"I've been trying to get her to lead, but she just fights it," Chris said.

Miranda saw the fear in Shooting Star's eyes when the rope tightened. The foal set her feet and shook her head, nearly pulling Chris off balance.

"Wait," Miranda said. "She's not used to it, and it's scaring her."

Chris scowled at Miranda and handed her the rope. "Fine, you do it. I wasn't hurting her!"

"I know. I didn't say you were. I just thought we could figure out a better way. When I started working with Starlight, I didn't try to force him; he was way too big and strong for me. Maybe if we try putting ourselves in her place we'll get an idea."

Miranda was stroking Shooting Star's face and neck. The little filly loved to be scratched and petted. She pushed against Miranda's hand. Miranda backed up a step and lowered her hand. Shooting Star stepped forward to fill in the space and nosed Miranda's hand. Miranda scratched her again for a moment and took two steps back. The foal quickly filled the gap and Miranda petted her some more. By repeating this action, Miranda steadily increased the distance, and Shooting Star quickly closed the gap.

"But you're not really leading her. She hasn't even felt the pull of the rope yet," Chris said.

"I know," Miranda agreed, "but it's a beginning. She's learning that she doesn't have to be afraid of the halter, at least."

"Big deal!" Chris exclaimed. "As soon as you try to pull her with the rope, she'll fight back, and you'll be just where I was."

"That's why I don't want to pull her," Miranda

said. "It scares her now, but if we give her time to get used to it, maybe it'll be different. Let's just do this every day for a while. When she follows us farther, we can give her treats. That way, she'll want to come with us and it will get to be a habit, not a fight."

"But Miranda, that's not really leading. It's just her getting her way. When she doesn't want to come, she won't, if we don't teach her that she doesn't have a choice," Chris argued.

"It wasn't that way with Starlight," Miranda said.

But somehow, little Shooting Star wasn't as interested in the treats as she was getting rid of the halter.

"See, Miranda?" Chris said, as Shooting Star shook her head.

"I didn't say it wouldn't take time," Miranda said. "But do whatever you want. I'm going to see if Dad's ready to go home."

As soon as Miranda got home, Margot ran to meet her.

"Miranda, come see what Sea Foam can do!"

Miranda followed Margot to the corral outside the old horse barn. Unfastening the lead rope from the halter, Margot walked in front of the little mare who followed with her muzzle against Margot's sleeve. When Margot trotted, so did Sea Foam.

"Wow, Margot!" Miranda exclaimed. "That's cool. She sure likes you."

"I've ridden her around the corral bareback, a little. But don't tell. I'm supposed to wait until I have a saddle and a helmet."

"The auction's tomorrow. Maybe Caruthers will have what you need," Miranda said.

"How much money do you have?"

"I won three thousand, one hundred fifty," Miranda said, "but not everyone has paid yet. I have two thousand in the bank, so far. That's a lot of money. Dad wants me to use at least that much of it to start a college fund, but would leave over a thousand after paying for Sea Foam if everyone would pay. So far I only have five hundred to spend."

At bedtime, the excitement of the upcoming day was replaced by a deep ache in Miranda's chest. She thought of Kort; her last vision of him crying for her to rescue him was vivid in her mind. They hadn't heard from Lorna Schoffler since she'd taken him away. She thought of Starlight's empty stall. Tears soaked her pillow until she fell into a fitful sleep filled with bad dreams. Mom woke her early to get ready for the sale.

The day was clear and sunny, but the wind that blew out of the north was bitter cold. When Miranda came in from doing her morning chores, she added a layer by putting a heavy sweat shirt under her school jacket. She and Margot were going to the sale with Dad and Grandpa. They'd be outside most of the day, and it could turn colder.

There were cars and pickup trucks lining the road for a quarter of a mile in both directions from the Caruthers' ranch house. A farm or ranch auction was more than just a place to buy used equipment; it was a social event.

"We might just as well have walked across the

pastures," Dad said. "We'd have gotten here almost as fast."

Miranda knew he was exaggerating. Though the Caruthers' place bordered Greene's dairy, there was a river pasture, a hay field, and three fences between Miranda's house and Caruthers' barnyard. By the road it was almost three miles.

In the open area between the house and the outbuildings, big tables, wagons, and the flat beds of a couple of trucks were piled with boxes, tools, and various odds and ends from the house, barns, and tool sheds. People were milling around, looking for things to buy. More tables were set up in the garage, where coffee and donuts were being served. Preparations for lunch were underway.

"Laurie!" Miranda shouted when she saw her friend walking up the driveway with her mother, each carrying a covered dish.

"Hi, Miranda," Laurie answered. "I thought you'd be here."

"Is your mother coming?" Mrs. Langley asked, as Miranda ran to meet them.

"Yes, she's coming with Grandma. They're bringing food for the potluck."

"Isn't this exciting?" Laurie asked. "I've never been to an auction before. It looks like everyone is here. Look, there's Bill. I haven't seen him in ages. Let's go talk to him."

Bill Meredith had been a classmate of Laurie and Miranda's until the previous year, when Laurie's father had begun teaching their sixth-grade class. Then his parents decided to home-school him for the rest of the year. When school started this year, Laurie had been very disappointed that he wasn't back in school. Miranda heard that he was enrolled in a smaller school in a neighboring town. It was so small, they didn't have enough students for their own basketball team, and so they played on the Country View team. Miranda had seen him at a home game, but Laurie hadn't been there.

As they hurried to catch up with Bill, Margot ran up behind them and grabbed Miranda's hand.

"Miranda, come look! There is a cool little cart in the barn. I think it's for sale," Margot exclaimed.

"Okay. I'll catch up with you and Bill later, Laurie."

The cart had two bicycle tires with a small box and a seat between. The front of it rested on two long

shafts spaced about three feet apart.

"It's made for a horse to pull, isn't it Miranda?" Margot asked.

"Yes! And it's very light," Miranda said, picking up the shafts and pulling it a few feet.

"Do you think Sea Foam could pull it?"

"Yes. It would probably be easier on her than carrying us on her back!" Miranda exclaimed. "I wonder how much it will go for. Of course, then we'd have to buy a harness too. Let's see if they have one."

The girls walked slowly through the barn. There were some old, well-worn Western saddles, several bridles, harnesses, collars and halters.

"We have to bid on this one!" Miranda exclaimed, examining a light harness. "I hope no one else wants it."

Bidding started with the boxes of tools and small implements that were on a flat bed trailer near the shop. Men crowded around, examining each item as the auctioneer started the bidding in a fast singsong voice that was hard to understand. Miranda soon lost interest and went looking for Laurie. Instead, she found Chris wandering around the barnyard, looking lonely and bored.

"Hi Chris, have you seen Laurie and Bill?"

"No, I haven't seen anyone. Where have you been?"

"Around. I've been trying to decide what I want to bid on," Miranda said proudly, holding up a card with a number on it.

She had registered for her own bid card when Dad and Grandpa had gotten theirs.

"Just don't get carried away with it," Grandpa had warned. "Once they take your bid, you're committed. With a nod or a wave you can buy something you don't even want."

Miranda showed Chris the barn where all the tack and the two-wheeled cart were stored. They closely examined bridles, halters, saddles, hoof picks, brushes, currycombs, liniment, and fly spray. They were all set out on a long, flat bench, ready to be sold.

"You don't need to buy any of this stuff, Miranda. Mr. Taylor lets you use whatever you want out of his tack shed," Chris said. "He has all this stuff and more."

"I know, but we need things for Sea Foam. Besides, someday I might bring Starlight here to live, and then I'll need my own tack," Miranda said.

"Why would you want to do that?"

"So I can be with him all the time. Someday he'll be all mine. Then I won't let anyone take him to any more races."

"If he was here, you couldn't ride with me and Laurie," Chris said.

"I can't anyway, with him in Texas or wherever Mr. Taylor decides to take him," Miranda said as tears filled her eyes.

She brushed them away quickly when she heard footsteps approaching.

"Oh, there you are. We've been looking all over for you," Laurie said.

Bill walked beside Laurie, holding her hand.

Chapter Twelve

Miranda stared at her friend, surprised to see her holding hands with a boy. She didn't quite understand the feelings that welled up inside her, but she didn't like them. She counted on Laurie's friendship. Bill seemed to pose a threat.

"Hi, Bill," Chris said. "Good to see you."

"I have an idea," Miranda said. "Let's play hide and seek. This is a cool old barn. It'll be fun to explore while we play. Not it!"

"Not it," echoed Bill and Laurie in unison.

"No fair!" Chris exclaimed. "I wasn't ready."

"Start counting and don't peek," Miranda said. "Come on, Laurie." They ran toward a far corner where some old cans and boxes provided a hiding place.

"Wait," Bill whispered.

"Go that way, Bill. We need to spread out so he can't find us all at once," Miranda whispered, grabbing

Laurie's hand and pulling her with her.

"What are you doing?" Miranda whispered as she and Laurie crouched behind some empty barrels.

"What do you mean?" Laurie asked.

"You were holding hands with Bill!"

"So?"

"Is he your boyfriend?"

"Maybe," Laurie said. "What if he is?"

"I didn't know you were interested in boys! I hope you don't get as silly as Kimberly and Stephanie."

"Liking a boy doesn't make me silly, Miranda. It's normal. After all, we're almost teenagers. All the other girls in our class are going out."

"Going out!" Miranda scoffed. "They get a crush on some boy and they say they're going out, when their parents would never let them go anywhere with a boy, even if the boys wanted to, which they don't."

"What makes you think you know so much about it?" Laurie asked. "You may be an expert about horses, but you sure don't know anything about boys."

"No, and I don't want to," Miranda said. "I'll take horses any day."

"So you don't want me to like Bill?"

"No, I don't mean that. I just never thought about you having a boyfriend. Are you in love?"

"I like him a lot, okay?" Laurie snapped.

"Sure it's okay. Just don't forget about our friendship," Miranda said, afraid that Laurie might.

"One, Two, Three on Miranda," Chris shouted. "You too, Laurie. If you don't want to be caught, you shouldn't talk so loud."

Miranda groaned and crawled out of her hiding place. She was "it" for the next game, but it really wasn't fun anymore. She found Laurie and Bill in the hayloft and couldn't find Chris at all until she called him to come in free. Finally the auctioneer and the crowd of men and women came into the barn. Margot met Miranda and stood close to her.

"I found a saddle I want, Miranda. It's the smallest one over there," Margot said, pointing. "See the black one with the cover things over the stirrups?"

Miranda nodded. "Yeah, I saw it, and there's a bridle in that pile that matches it."

The bidding started with a box of odds and ends.

"Every accessory you need for grooming your livestock!" hawked the auctioneer. "If you have youngsters showing horses or cattle at the fair, here's all they need to get ready."

He held up a pair of clippers and a currycomb, dropped them back into the box and picked up a brush.

"We don't have any of that stuff, Miranda," Margot reminded her.

The bidding started at five dollars and Miranda raised her hand to bid six. No one seemed to notice her, however, and the bidding went back and forth between three different men, until one of them dropped out at fifteen dollars. Miranda kept waving her hand, angry that not one of the auctioneer's helpers paid the least bit of attention.

"Sixteen, I've got sixteen, gimme twenty," the auctioneer chanted.

Finally Miranda pulled her bid card from her
pocket and held it high over her head,'

"Twenty, I've got twenty—the young lady in the
blue coat, do I hear twenty-five?"

"Twenty-one," shouted one of the helpers.

"Twenty-one! Thank you, Mr. Miller. Now
twenty-five?" roared the auctioneer, looking straight at
Miranda.

She nodded as she had seen the men do.

"Yes!" one of the helpers yelled.

"I've got twenty-five, do I hear thirty? Gimme thirty, thirty, thirty," the auctioneer sang, pointing toward Mr. Miller.

"Sold!" he shouted, pointing to Miranda. "To number 54 for twenty-five dollars."

"We bought it!" Miranda said excitedly, hugging Margot.

"Why was Grandpa shaking his head at us?" Margot asked. "Didn't he want us to get it?"

Miranda looked up to see Grandpa coming through the crowd toward them.

"We got it, Grandpa," Miranda told him.

"I saw that," he said with a smile.

"Did I do something wrong?"

"Oh, no. I would have suggested you wait, but that's okay."

"Why wait?"

"Well, there are a couple more boxes with similar items, which might sell cheaper, but then again they might not."

Miranda looked up to see the bidding close on the next box, sold to Mr. Miller for seventeen dollars.

"Just save your money for the things you want the most, and don't pay more than you could get them for in a store," Grandpa advised as he touched her shoulder and walked away.

"Let's go stand by the saddle you want," Miranda said, taking Margot by the hand.

As she turned to leave she nearly bumped into Mrs. Meredith.

"Oh, excuse me," Miranda said, turning to go around her.

"Wait, you're Kathy Greene's granddaughter, aren't you?" Mrs. Meredith asked. "Have you seen my son, Bill?"

"Uh, yes. I saw him earlier, but I don't know where he is now."

"Well if you see him, tell him to come to the garage to find me. I want to go home."

"Okay," Miranda said, hurrying away.

Miranda didn't like Mrs. Meredith because the woman made it no secret that she didn't like the Langleys. *She probably wants to leave because Laurie and her mom are here*, Miranda thought. Mr. Langley hadn't come, choosing to stay home and grade papers.

There were several people in the community who had been very slow in accepting the Langleys' presence in the community. Mr. Langley's African heritage was obvious. Some people were just plain prejudiced, and there were many who felt that his marriage to a blonde, blue-eyed woman was nothing less than a sin. Miranda couldn't understand that kind of thinking, and her temper quickly flared when anyone said anything against her best friend or her family.

The bidding opened on a saddle that was far too big for either Margot or Miranda. Margot lost interest and went to find Elliot.

"I'll be back before they get to my saddle," she said, as if the small black one already belonged to her.

Miranda watched with dismay as the bidding shot from two hundred dollars to over five hundred.

That was more money than she had left to spend. She had felt so rich when she'd arrived with five hundred dollars in the wallet that she kept fingering in the bottom of her pocket. Now she only had four hundred seventy-five left, and she still wanted to buy at least one saddle and bridle, a harness and the cart. She wondered if anyone who owed her money would be willing to pay her today.

"Sold, six seventy-five, to number 12, Jerry Huston," the auctioneer shouted before moving on to the next saddle.

It was older and the leather was curled in places. It sold for three-fifty.

"Now here is a nice little saddle, perfect for kids or petite ladies. Notice the hand-tooled leather. It has hardly been used and all the rigging is like new. Who'll start the bid for me? Who'll give me two hundred?"

"One hundred," yelled a voice from the crowd.

"One hundred, who'll give me two? One-fifty, I've got one-fifty, will you give me two?"

Before Miranda could raise her hand, the first bidder had nodded. The second raised it another fifty and soon it was three hundred. Miranda waved her card in the air.

"Three fifty!" shouted the auctioneer. "Will you give four hundred . . . Yes!" And the bidding continued to five hundred in seconds. The auctioneer tried to get her to bid, and then sold it for five hundred twenty five, to . . . Miranda searched the crowd to see.

Mrs. Meredith! A wave of anger surged through Miranda. Mr. Meredith was one of the people who still hadn't paid his pledge for the race. Miranda was unable to get Margot her saddle, all because of the Merediths!

The bidding moved to the bridles, and Miranda bid on several, but always stopped at twenty dollars. When the auctioneer held up a black headstall with a snaffle bit that looked like it would fit Sea Foam, she decided to go a little higher. There was only one other bridle left and it wasn't nearly as pretty as the black one. She smiled with relief when the bidding stopped at thirty dollars and the bridle was hers.

"Miranda, come quick!" Chris Bergman shouted, as he pulled on Miranda's arm.

"What? I can't come now. They will be selling the harness soon, or the buggy," Miranda protested. "I have to stay here."

"It's Laurie. She's in the hayloft. She's crying and she won't tell me why."

The hayloft was dim and dusty. Miranda couldn't see anyone. She was about to go back down the ladder when she heard a sniffle.

"Laurie?" she asked softly.

There was no answer, and Miranda walked slowly in the direction of the sound. She found her friend slumped against a pile of moldy hay, wiping tears from her eyes.

"What's the matter? Did you get hurt?" Miranda asked in alarm.

"No, I just got yelled at like I'm some kind of wicked, devil woman," Laurie sobbed.

"Who yelled at you? What did they say?" Miranda asked indignantly.

"Bill's mother. She came storming up here and started yelling. She grabbed Bill by the arm and told him to stay away from me. She called me some really nasty names and told me to stay away from her son," Laurie said, crying again. "Then she yelled at him about not being able to trust him and said if she ever caught him with me again, she'd lock him in his room and throw away the key."

"That..." Miranda bit her tongue. "She is such a witch! Remember how nice she was to you when you helped her after her car wreck. She said the nicest things about you and wanted to give you a reward until she found out who your father is. I think she's the only one in town who still hates your family just because of the color of your dad's skin!"

"Oh, there are a few others. It's so unfair! I really like Bill. We were just sitting here talking. We weren't doing anything wrong, Miranda, I swear."

"I know that! Just ignore Mrs. Meredith. She's probably just jealous that her son likes you so much."

"I like him a lot, too. I hope that doesn't make you mad at me. I want to be your friend," Laurie said.

"No, I'm not mad at you," Miranda said, holding Laurie's hand. "I guess I just got worried that I'd lose my best friend when I saw you holding his hand."

"You won't. I can like both of you. Bill is nothing like his parents and he wants to come back to Country View really bad," Laurie said. "He thinks his father would let him, but his dad won't argue with his mom. I probably won't ever get to see him again."

"Well, that's not fair. She must not love her son very much, or she'd let him choose his own friends," Miranda said, reaching for Laurie's hand. "Let's go to her store after school Monday. She told you to come by and she'd give you something, remember? After the car wreck?"

"I don't want to go to her store! She'd kick me out!" Laurie exclaimed. "I don't ever want to see her again!"

"You want to see Bill, don't you?"

"Yes, but . . ."

"Then we'll go talk to her. We'll make her explain herself and we'll make her listen!" Miranda urged.

Miranda rushed back to the old barn but the crowd had moved away. The harness and the two-wheeled cart had numbers on them. She had missed the chance to bid on them.

By mid-afternoon, it was beginning to snow and the wind had gotten stronger. The crowd was thinning as, one by one, people hurried to their vehicles and drove away. The auctioneer was inside the machine shed, selling tractors and implements. Dad and Grandpa were there.

"When are we going home?" Miranda asked.

"Soon. I want to see if I can get the swather and baler," Dad said. "Your Grandpa's are about worn out and we have quite a bit of hay ground now. I'll be able to provide all the hay for your grandfather's cows and he won't have to haul it from Millers' anymore."

Miranda went to the garage where Mom and Grandma were still serving sloppy joes, chili, and coffee. Several women stood behind the big table, laughing and talking to their neighbors as they served them hot food. Miranda sat down to wait, suddenly feeling very tired.

The girls sat at the table doing homework after supper. Margot had withdrawn into her shell, sullen with disappointment. After an attempt to explain that it wasn't her fault she didn't get harness, buggy, or saddle, Miranda had given up and was concentrating on her books. The phone rang and Margot jumped up to get it before Miranda could.

"It's for you, Miranda," Margot said. "It's Colton."

Chapter Thirteen

Eager for news of Starlight, Miranda rushed to the phone.

"Hello?"

"Miranda, it's Colton. Just wanted to let you know we're all safe and sound at the Taylor ranch."

"How's Starlight?" Miranda asked.

"He's fine. We stopped and walked him pretty often; made sure he had plenty of water. It sure is hot down here for October!"

"Does he miss me?"

"Sure he does. But I'm doing my best to take care of him. He's in the nicest stall in the stables, but even so, I had to clean it before I could put him in. This place is really run down. It's hard to believe anyone related to Mr. Taylor could let a place get into such a mess."

"Really? What's it like? Does it look anything like Shady Hills?"

"It's big, and Mr. Taylor said it was the nicest looking place in South Texas when he lived there. It's laid out a lot like Shady Hills, only bigger. You know the stable row at Shady Hills? Well, multiply that by three. The indoor arena also has stalls along both sides. The fences are all rotted and falling over. The windows on the house have been boarded up, but evidently not soon enough. The place is trashed, and there is graffiti spray painted all over the walls."

"Oh, no! Mr. Taylor must be very upset!"

"That's putting it mildly. He said there was some very expensive antique furniture that he hoped to inherit. It's all gone. There's not even a stove or refrigerator in there!"

"So I suppose you're sleeping in the trailer," Miranda said, thinking of the camper-like living quarters in the front of the horse van.

"No, we're at a motel. After the long trip, we were ready for hot running water and a telephone."

"But what about Starlight?" Miranda asked in alarm. "Someone could come steal him!"

"I left Lucky out at the ranch. He'll bark if anyone comes around."

"Yeah, sure! And then what, lick them to death? Beat them up with his tail wagging? You know Lucky is no watch dog."

"I'll put him in the stable with Starlight. We can even put a padlock on the door, if that makes you feel better."

"People can cut padlocks or break down rotten walls. If they stole everything out of the house, how do you know they won't steal a racehorse?"

"Well, I have to admit I was a little worried my-self. Now that I've showered and eaten, I'll go back and check on him. I can park the trailer right in front of his door and sleep there. Then I'll be sure to hear Lucky bark if anyone comes around."

"Oh, thank you, Colton. Keep a really close eye on him, would you. I would die if anything happened to him."

"I promise, Miranda."

The days were long and sad for Miranda. She wished Colton would call every day, but a whole week went by without hearing from him again. On the week-end, Miranda helped Margot with Sea Foam. Mar was riding bareback as Miranda longed, led and backed the little horse around the barnyard. She cleaned out her chicken coop and rabbit hutches, as well as her regular chores. Keeping busy made waiting a little easier.

Laurie wasn't in school on Monday. When Miranda called her house, Mrs. Langley answered.

"She's sleeping right now, Miranda. She has one of her bad colds again. I think she could have gone to school, but she really didn't want to. She's been weak and tired and sleeping a lot."

"Could I come see her?" Miranda asked. "I could bring her homework."

"Sure, if you aren't afraid of catching a cold. I think it would do Laurie good to have some company."

Laurie was up and dressed when Miranda got there. She had a stopped-up nose and her eyes were a little red, but otherwise she seemed to feel fine.

"I brought all the books I could find in your locker," Miranda said. "Do you have your history book?"

"Yeah, I brought it home Friday."

"We're going to have a test over chapter eight tomorrow. I can study with you if you want. The math is kind of hard. It's algebra, but its fun. Sort of like breaking a code, or solving a puzzle," Miranda said. "I can show you what Mr. Larson showed us on the board today."

The girls sat at the polished table in the spacious dining room. A fire crackled in the fireplace that opened into both the living room and dining room. Miranda loved Laurie's house. It was elegant, but cozy and inviting. Laurie caught on to the math quickly, and they soon proceeded to the short English assignment, and then studied History. It was about the Civil War.

After reading the Emancipation Proclamation, Laurie sighed and closed her book.

"What?" Miranda asked. "Don't you think Lincoln did a good thing?"

"Sure," Laurie agreed. "It's just sad that it needed to be done. I don't understand how some people can think it's all right to treat other people like they aren't even human. What is it about skin color that makes such a difference?"

"People that think that way are stupid and mean. It makes me really mad. You know that, Laurie."

"I know, but look how many people still think that way," Laurie said, wiping a tear from her eye. "Remember when we studied the Revolutionary War and the Declaration of Independence?"

"Yeah, why?"

"In 1776 it was written, 'We hold these truths to be self-evident, that all men are created equal, that they are endowed by their Creator with certain unalienable Rights, that among these are Life, Liberty and the pursuit of Happiness.'"

"Wow, you memorized that?"

"Yes! It's beautiful and it's true. But the sad thing is it didn't keep people from kidnapping Africans and forcing them to work as slaves in a strange country separated from their families. And it took, let's see . . ." Laurie picked up her pencil and scribbled on a piece of scratch paper. "It took eighty-seven years before anyone tried to do anything about it. It was eighty-nine years from the time men said 'all men are created equal,' before any slaves were actually set free after the Civil War ended."

"I never thought of that."

"But no matter what our presidents might say, or what wars are won and laws are made, you can't change people's ideas. Mrs. Meredith and a whole lot of others still look at anyone with black skin as if they were some form of low-life, and it doesn't matter what we do."

"I still say we should go talk to her. Make her explain what she has against you," Miranda said.

"No! It wouldn't change anything. It would just make me feel worse."

The phone rang while the girls were doing the supper dishes, and this time, Miranda beat Margot to answer it.

"Hello? Colton, I thought it was you. How's Starlight?"

"Umm, he's okay," Colton said. "Mr. Taylor signed us up for a race this weekend."

"What's wrong?" Miranda asked. "You aren't telling me the truth about Starlight! I can tell by your voice."

Miranda waited for several seconds for Colton to reply, thinking that something terrible had happened to her horse. Had there been an accident? She could hardly breathe.

"No, he's fine; just a little off his feed. Mr. Taylor said it's nothing to worry about. He says it's because I'm not exercising him enough, but then he gives me a dozen other jobs to do, so I don't have time for half of them."

"What do you mean off his feed. Is he eating at all? Does he act all right otherwise?"

"Well, Mr. Taylor didn't want me saying anything to worry you, and I didn't mean to, but he acts, well, sad. Kind of mopes around and looks off in the distance a lot. I think he misses you," Colton admitted, "but don't tell Mr. Taylor I told you. I'm sorry. I didn't want to worry you either."

"I'm glad you told me, but I wish there was something I could do about it." Tears welled up in Miranda's eyes. "I miss him, too. Please take good care of him, and tell him I love him."

Miranda fought back her tears until Margot was asleep that night. For once she wished she had her own room. Margot, who was still plagued with nightmares, had declined having her own room in the big new house, after talking Miranda into letting her sleep with her. When Miranda finally heard Margot snoring, she turned over, sobbed into her pillow and cried herself to sleep.

When she awoke the next morning, the ground was blanketed with six inches of snow. Miranda dressed quickly. She loved the snow and hurried out into it. She fed her chickens and rabbits, put the dogs' dishes in the shed and filled them with fresh food and water. Margot usually did that job, but she hadn't come out of the house yet. As Miranda walked from the shed past Grandma and Grandpa's house, she saw the fat old cat, Gleason, trying to get in the back door.

"Here, Gleason," Miranda said, stooping to pet him. "I'll let you in."

"Is that you, Miranda?" Grandma called when she opened the door.

"Yes, Gram. How do you like the snow?"

"Not as much as you do, I'm sure, especially when I have to drive to Bozeman."

"Why are you going to Bozeman?"

"Didn't your Mom tell you? She had a doctor's appointment. I'm going with her to get some groceries. If it keeps snowing though, maybe we'll cancel," Grandma said.

When Miranda reached her own house, Mom came out of the bedroom looking tired and a little pale.

"What's the matter, Mom? Are you sick?"

"I'm not feeling so well. I just threw up!"

"Oh! I'm sorry. What's wrong?"

"I'm not sure, but I bet I'll feel better after I have a little breakfast," Mom said, looking through the cupboards. "Oh, Laurie called while you were out. She wants you to come to her house after school. It's all right with me if you want to."

It snowed lightly throughout the day, but it wasn't very cold and the wind wasn't blowing. By the time school was out, the snow was wet and sloppy as it slowly melted. Laurie and Miranda sloshed through it, enjoying the splat of each step on her way to Laurie's house. They stopped in front of the Antique Shoppe, surprised to see that it was open. Mrs. Meredith usually closed it except on weekends during the winter, when there wasn't much traffic going through town.

"Let's go in," Miranda said. "Remember when you helped her after her car wreck? She told you to come in some time and pick out something from her store."

"No way, Miranda. I told you I'm not going in there! Besides not wanting to see her, I don't take pay for being nice to people," Laurie said. "Besides, that was a long time ago, and you know what she thinks of me now."

"Yeah, but I don't know why! One day she thinks you're the greatest girl on earth, and then decides you're not even good enough to be around her precious son," Miranda fumed. "You didn't change! I'd like to hear her explain what made her change her mind."

"Then you ask her some time when I'm not with

you; I don't want to hear it."

A loud crash from inside the shop caused both girls to jump.

"Stupid! Ohhhh, owww," came from the interior of the shop.

Miranda and Laurie dashed in and found Mrs. Meredith lying on the floor underneath a ladder.

"Quick, Miranda, help me lift this ladder," Laurie said. "Let's go straight up with it so we don't bump her."

As soon as the ladder was moved out of the way, Laurie knelt beside Mrs. Meredith and peered into her eyes.

"Where do you hurt, Mrs. Meredith?" Laurie's voice was gentle. "No, don't try to move! You might have a broken bone somewhere."

"I'm so cold. I can't lie here on this cold floor!" Mrs. Meredith whined. "Oh, my head hurts!"

"Should I call for help?" Miranda asked.

"Yes, and see if you can find a blanket," Laurie said. "I think she's in shock."

Mrs. Meredith lay with her eyes closed for several minutes, moaning softly as the girls tucked a thick woolen blanket around her.

"The ambulance is on the way," Miranda told Laurie.

"What happened?" Mrs. Meredith asked, staring at the girls who leaned over her.

"The ladder must have fallen with you. We heard the crash as we were walking by," Miranda said.

"Oh, yes. I was trying to get that porcelain basin

off the top shelf. A customer phoned and told me she was looking for one. I should have gotten down and moved the ladder closer, but I thought I could reach it."

"Do you hurt anywhere besides your head?" Laurie asked.

"I hurt everywhere! And this hard floor isn't helping."

"I know. I'm sorry, but until we know for sure

you haven't broken your back, it would be very dangerous to move you. The ambulance will be here soon." Laurie said.

"You're the Langley girl, aren't you?" Mrs. Meredith asked, squinting. "It seems that every time I get hurt, you're right there, helping me. You ought to be a nurse or a doctor when you grow up."

"I'm surprised to hear you say that," Miranda interjected. "I thought you hated Laurie because she's part African American! Would you go to a black doctor?"

Laurie shot Miranda a warning glance. "This isn't the time . . . " she began.

"And you're Kathy Greene's granddaughter! You need to take some lessons from your friend!" Mrs. Meredith said. "It wouldn't hurt you to be a little kinder to an injured woman!"

"Kinder? I don't want to be mean, but you hurt Laurie's feelings when you told her she can't be friends with your son!"

Chapter Fourteen

"Miranda," Laurie said, "Not now. Mrs. Meredith, do you want us to call your family?"

"Here comes the ambulance," Miranda said. "That was fast."

"Yes, please call home. Just push memory, and then one," Mrs. Meredith said. "I don't think my husband will be in the house, but Bill might. Tell him what happened."

"I will," Miranda said.

"Here are the paramedics, I'll get out of the way," Laurie said.

"Wait!" Mrs. Meredith said, grasping Laurie's hand. "Thank you! I appreciate your help, both of you."

"You're welcome," Laurie said.

Miranda waited, wishing Mrs. Meredith would apologize to Laurie, but the medics were kneeling beside her, asking questions and preparing to move her onto a back board.

"Good bye, Mrs. Meredith. I hope you get well soon," Laurie said as the girls headed for the door.

"Uh, wait," Mrs. Meredith called. "I want you both to know you're welcome to come back anytime."

Laurie turned, looked sadly at Mrs. Meredith, and spoke softly.

"Mrs. Meredith, thank you, but as long as you think I'm not good enough to be around your son, I don't think I'll want to visit your store. Bill and I didn't do anything wrong. I'm not a bad person and I'm sure you know Bill isn't either."

"Stop!" Mrs. Meredith shouted to the medics as they lifted her onto the gurney. "I need to talk to this girl. Laurie, come here!"

Miranda watched Laurie hesitate, brushing away a tear before going to Mrs. Meredith's side.

"I apologize, Laurie," Mrs. Meredith said. "I know you're not a bad person. You've always been especially good to me, even after I was unkind to you. I guess Bill couldn't find a nicer friend, and I know he thinks so."

"Thank you," Laurie said, squeezing Mrs. Meredith's hand.

A bitter wind out of the north brought snow to the Montana landscape in mid-November. For three weeks, through a dismal Thanksgiving and into December, clouds obscured the sun, and powder-fine snow streaked horizontally, leaving drifts piled in corners and across roads. The bleak barren ground was swept clean between the drifts.

Miranda's mood matched the landscape as the days drearily dragged on. Colton rarely called anymore, and Miranda guessed it was because Mr. Taylor didn't want him "worrying" her. But with thoughts of Kort and of Starlight, she worried herself sick. She finally convinced herself that Starlight had died, and neither Colton nor Mr. Taylor wanted to tell her. And what about Kort? If he was all right, why didn't Lorna call?

On the morning of December fifteenth, a bright sun streamed into her bedroom window and woke her. It was Saturday and she had slept late, for she hated to face another weekend without Starlight. Getting up was becoming harder every day.

"Are you awake, Miranda?" Margot yelled, jumping on the bed and pulling back the covers. "A fancy car just drove up. I think it's Kort's mom."

Miranda dressed quickly, and ran to the living room. Lorna Schoffler was standing in the entry way, holding Kort in her arms.

"Kort!" Miranda shouted, running to take him from Lorna.

Kort looked a little confused or scared for a moment and then leaned toward her. He hugged her neck as she held him and walked into the living room.

"I brought him back," Lorna said, simply. "I can't deal with trying to work and take care of him. He's been so moody, I can't keep a good nanny!"

"Is he okay?" asked Mom. "We've been worried sick about him, and we couldn't get hold of you."

"He's fine, but I think he missed you. I believe

he'll be better off here. I guess I shouldn't have taken him so abruptly. I'll go get his things."

"Oh, no! I don't think that's going to work, Ms. Schoffler," Dad said.

Miranda stared at him as if she thought he'd lost his mind. Lorna turned and stared, mouth wide open.

"What do you mean?"

"As much as I love Kort and want to give him a good home, I can't be part of a roller-coaster ride that will leave him broken and bitter."

"But Barry," Mom said, looking up from the floor where she knelt in front of Miranda, holding Kort's hand and looking him over carefully.

Ignoring her, Dad continued. "When you took him away without a moment's notice, you not only broke the heart of everyone in this household, you also upset a three-year-old who had no way of understanding why he was ripped from the people he loved most. I can't stand to see that happen again in a few months or years."

"It won't happen again. I've learned my lesson. I have a leading role in a major film. I'll be traveling from one location to another. I can't take care of him. I want him to be with people he loves."

"Then sign the adoption papers."

Lorna looked stunned for a moment and then opened her large handbag.

"I brought them with me. I have had them signed and notarized."

Dad took the papers and looked them over.

"I guess everything is official then. You can't go back on this, Lorna."

"You may visit him," Mom said. "Just call ahead and let us know. But we won't let you take him away from us again. Is that perfectly clear?"

"Yes, Carey. I swear. I've made my final choice. It's better for both of us. I love Kort and I can't make him happy. You can."

Miranda was absorbed with Kort during the days that followed, playing with him, feeding him, taking him outdoors to see the wonders of nature and all the animals on the farm. She showed him tracks that deer, rabbits and squirrels left in the snow. But at night, after Kort was tucked into bed, the heartsickness and worry over Starlight kept her awake until she cried herself to exhaustion.

The following Saturday she awoke with such a feeling of dread that she burrowed deeper into the covers and tried to go back to sleep.

"Miranda?" Mom called from the doorway to her room. "Telephone for you. I think it's Colton."

Miranda sat up quickly and snatched the cordless phone from her mother's hand.

"Hello? Colton? Is Starlight okay?" Miranda couldn't breathe, dreading the terrible news that her beloved horse had died far away without her.

"Yeah, he's okay, except . . ." Colton paused for so long that Miranda thought he'd been disconnected.

"Colton? Are you there?"

"Yes. I just, well, do you think there's any way you can come down here over your Christmas break?"

"Why? Colton, tell me what's wrong this minute. You're scaring me!" Miranda shouted. She felt more frightened than she could remember ever feeling before.

"It's just that he won't eat. Mr. Taylor has had all kinds of horse doctors look at him and do blood tests and everything. He's lost a lot of weight. I finally convinced Mr. Taylor that it's because he misses you. One vet told him that I could be right, because they can't find anything else wrong with him."

Miranda wanted to get on an airplane that minute and go to her horse before it was too late. Her parents said that was impossible, but that they would see about getting tickets. Mom didn't like the idea of having Miranda gone over the holidays.

"Why doesn't Mr. Taylor just bring Starlight home?" she wanted to know.

"I think he's too sick to travel," Miranda said. "He'll die if I don't go."

Dad talked to Mr. Taylor for a long time that night, before he got on the phone to the airlines and tried to find a flight out for her. The airlines were booked until after Christmas.

"See?" Miranda heard her mother say. "It isn't meant to be. I don't like having her traveling alone this time of year. And I certainly don't want her down in Texas with two men . . ."

"Carey, honey," Dad interrupted, pulling his wife into his arms. "Mr. Taylor's a decent, responsible man, and he'll take good care of her. I've been worried about her lately. Haven't you noticed that she's been off her feed, too, and getting paler and thinner every passing day?"

"Of course I've noticed," Mom replied. "That's all the more reason I don't want her to go."

"I know how you feel, Carey. I'll worry about her too, but I'm convinced that neither Miranda nor her horse is going to get better until they're together."

"Isn't that a little superstitious?" Mom asked, looking up.

Miranda quickly backed out of the doorway before her mother saw that she was listening.

The whole family, including Grandma and Grandpa, accompanied Miranda to the airport Wednesday morning. Dad had standby tickets for her and for himself, in case two seats became available at the last minute. If there were only one, Miranda would go alone. It was the last day of school before Christmas break, and Margot had the choice of going to the class parties, or coming to the airport. She chose the latter. The small airport terminal was getting very boring, for nobody canceled his or her morning flight.

"I guess you should have gone to school," Miranda said to her as they sat in the terminal, watching Kort play on the floor beside them.

"That's okay. I'd rather spend the day with you. I'll miss you," Margot said.

They had two more hours to wait for the next flight to depart. There were no cancellations on it, either.

At 7:50 p.m. Delta flight 1254 was making a final boarding call over the PA system. In a few minutes a voice boomed again, "Will Joseph Atkins please report to Gate 2 for final boarding. Joseph Atkins, your plane is departing."

Miranda stood up and Dad took her hand as they walked the short distance to Gate 2. The attendant put up his hand.

"We'll give him another minute," he said before calling the name into the microphone again. "Guess he's not coming," he finally said. "Let's have your ticket."

Miranda had to wait in Denver for a flight attendant to take her to her next plane; her mom had insisted they pay the extra fee for assistance for an unaccompanied minor.

After a long layover, during which she had to wait in a room with a few other children, watching TV, reading books, and playing some games, she was finally escorted to another plane bound for Houston. It was nearly five o'clock in the morning when she was finally taken to the baggage claim where Colton and Mr. Taylor awaited her. Miranda was so relieved to see them that she hugged them both.

The ride to Mr. Taylor's family ranch would have seemed interminable if Miranda hadn't fallen asleep as soon as she nestled against Colton's arm in the Shady Hills Ranch pickup. A blow to her shoulder and a wet tongue on her face jolted Miranda awake. She pushed at something furry, opened her eyes, and stared into the eager black eyes and panting mouth of Colton's dog.

"Sorry," Colton said, pulling Lucky out by the collar. "He jumped in as soon as I opened the door."

Miranda sat up and looked out. The sun was a large red ball sitting on the flat eastern horizon. The pickup was parked in front of a large Colonial-style house, badly in need of a fresh coat of paint.

"Where's Starlight?" she asked.

"I'll take you to him," Colton answered, reaching for her hand to help her out of the truck.

Her first glimpse of Starlight made her stomach ache. He stood, head down, in the corner of a dim stall. Every rib stood out and his coat had lost all of its shine. He gave no sign that he heard them when Colton spoke to him.

"Starlight, I have a surprise for you. She's here; your Miranda. Look!"

Miranda stared for a moment, tears clouding her eyes, unable to speak. Slowly she walked to his head, threw her arms around his neck, and sobbed. Starlight raised his head slowly and Miranda stepped back. He looked at her, closed his eyes, and rested his head against her chest.

Miranda spent the entire day with Starlight, leading him into the big yard under the bright Texas sun. She marveled at how warm it was. No need for a jacket; the lawn was green and looked as if it needed mowing. She brushed Starlight gently, fed him oat cubes, and let him graze in the large yard around the house.

"I guess Colton was right. All Starlight needed was a good dose of Miranda. I can't believe the difference. Look how he holds his head up, and this is the first time I've seen him eat in a long time," Mr. Taylor said as he came out the front door.

"Why didn't you call me sooner?" Miranda demanded. "He could have died before I got here!"

"I guess I just didn't believe a horse could pine to death over a person," Mr. Taylor said. "I thought it had to be something else, and I was determined to have him in good shape before you saw him again."

"How much longer are you staying here?" Miranda asked.

"Don't know for sure. I've got to sell this place, but no one wants it the way it is."

Miranda looked around. She could see that it had once been an elegant, high-class estate. It had acres of lawn and big barns, including two big enough to be indoor riding arenas. There were rows and rows of stables with divided paddocks behind each one, just like the ones Mr. Taylor had built at Shady Hills, which were unlike any others she had seen in Montana. But the fences had rotted and fallen over, and the doors drooped on one hinge or were completely missing on some of the outbuildings and stalls of the stable rows. Wagons and machinery in one long shed were rusted and had flat tires.

"You should have seen it when we first got here," Mr. Taylor said. "We've done a lot so far, mostly to the house. By the way, there is a racetrack out behind that barn."

Miranda led Starlight to the racetrack. As she led him past the empty bleachers, Starlight quickened his pace and lifted his head as if looking for the crowd in the stands.

"What are you thinking? You'd like to race again? Well, you can forget that idea until you've put some meat on those bones. I won't even get on you until you gain a little weight," Miranda said as she stopped and patted Starlight's face.

Starlight ate eagerly now. Mr. Taylor cautioned Miranda not to let him gorge himself. When Miranda finally put him back in his stall, kissed his nose and walked away, he went to the door and nickered softly, as if begging her to stay. She turned back and stroked his neck.

"Starlight, I feel the same way you do. I don't ever want to let you out of my sight again, but I've got to eat something, and Mr. Taylor insists I come in before he goes to bed. I'll be back first thing in the morning."

It took every ounce of willpower to tear herself away and go into the house. She had only been inside once, to use the bathroom while Colton held Starlight just outside the door. Now she looked around the house with curiosity. It was clean and neat, with new paint on the walls and new carpeting in the living room. It was sparsely furnished. Miranda sat at a built-in breakfast nook, like a booth in a restaurant, as Colton set a bowl of chicken noodle soup in front of her.

"And here's a sandwich," he said. "I hope you like it."

Miranda ate hungrily and took the second helping of soup that Colton offered her. Mr. Taylor said good night before she was finished and told her Colton would show her where she was to sleep.

The room looked very big, with a small cot in one corner. There was one small dresser, and her suitcase stood in front of it.

"This was Mr. Taylor's room when he was a boy. The furniture was all missing when we got here, but he found this cot at a secondhand store, so you'd have something to sleep on while you were here," Colton explained.

Miranda tossed and turned on the small cot. It was stuffy in the room. She got up to open the window but it was stuck tight. Finally she gave up. Unable to sleep, she took a blanket and crept out the door. Lucky lay asleep on the porch and didn't even hear her.

Chapter Fifteen

Miranda couldn't tell if Starlight was asleep or not as he stood, head down, in the corner of his stall. When she closed the door behind her, his head came up abruptly and he turned toward her, with a soft welcoming neigh rumbling deep in his throat. She petted him for a long time, leaning into his chest and weeping. It was such a relief to be with him again, that she couldn't hold back the tears. Finally she shoveled out some litter, put down clean shavings and spread her blanket over them. She lay down, exhausted. Starlight nuzzled her and then lowered himself, bending first his front legs, dropping to his knees, then flopping down beside her. Miranda placed her hand on his foreleg and fell into a deep sleep.

When Miranda awoke, Starlight was standing in the corner of the stall, munching on hay. Sunlight streamed into the open half of the stall door. She turned

over and stretched, smiling as she remembered that she was finally reunited with her horse.

"Starlight," she whispered. "Good morning, most beautiful creature in all the world."

Starlight turned away from his manger of hay and stepped toward Miranda. As she stood to meet him, he pressed his head against her, and she stroked his face, ears and neck.

"It's good to see you, too. I would have come

sooner if I could have. We must never let people separate us again!"

Starlight raised his head and craned his neck toward the door. Miranda followed his gaze and saw Colton and Mr. Taylor.

"Did you sleep out here?" Colton asked.

Miranda nodded.

"Don't you go sneaking out of the house again, young lady!" Mr. Taylor scolded. "I had to promise your mother that I'd keep an eye on you every minute, or she would never have let you come. The horse could have stepped on you while you were sleeping."

"Starlight would never do that!" Miranda said. "He's smart. He knows where I am and he would never hurt me."

"Maybe not," Mr. Taylor said, "but there are other dangers. Just look at the vandalism that's been done to this place. Someone comes back to do some more looting, sees you, and you could be kidnapped or murdered!"

"She's probably safer with Starlight than anywhere, in that case," Colton said. "I'd hate to see what was left of the guy that tried to harm Miranda when Starlight was around."

"Well, I have to admit, I've seen an example of that. Starlight put one attacker away for good."

Miranda leaned against Starlight, remembering the frightening night when a man had tried to kill Starlight, and when Miranda intervened, had threatened to kill her too. She and Starlight had been through some frightening times together, which only made them love each other more.

Miranda spent the day grooming, feeding and exercising Starlight. She planned to ride him on the track in the afternoon, but the unseasonable temperature made it too hot to ride.

"I'm going into the house for some iced tea," Colton said as he left the fence he was repairing. "You want to come?"

"No, since Starlight can't come in the house, I'll find a shady place where we can both be cool," Miranda said.

"It's the humidity, not the heat that's bothering you," Colton explained. "You're used to Montana's dry air. You oughta see Texas in the summertime."

"No thanks!" Miranda exclaimed.

She opened the door to an indoor riding arena and found it was just as warm inside. Next she tried the big old barn at the end of the driveway. Inside, the air was cooler, as the small windows were covered with boards nailed to the outside, and the big loft provided protection from the sun. After her eyes adjusted to the darkness, she led Starlight along a walkway between open stalls on each side. There were sixteen stalls altogether, each one big enough for two horses. They all had mangers, with a wooden grain box for each horse.

Miranda left Starlight in the farthest stall and went through a small door at the end of the walkway. There she found a small room with a metal cot frame, a broken chair and several racks for saddles, all empty. There were many hooks on the wall, but nothing hung on them. Either everything had been removed before

Mr. Taylor's parents had moved out, or the vandals and thieves had taken them.

Returning to Starlight, Miranda looked for a way to get into the hayloft. She could see an opening where hay could be thrown down into the mangers, but no ladder leading up to it.

"You wait here, Starlight," Miranda said. "I'll be right back."

She went outside and looked for another entrance into the barn. She found two. One was a huge sliding door, big enough for a large truck to go through. But it was off its track, with the bottom corner of one end buried in the ground. The other entrance was a regular-size opening, with the door leaning against the side of the barn nearby. It looked as if it had been ripped off its hinges and set aside.

Miranda began to sense how Mr. Taylor must feel to find everything stripped from his parents' ranch and destruction left in its wake. What fun it would have been to explore this place before the looters got to it!

A large desk lay on its side. The empty drawers were scattered about the small room. Miranda went through a door on the other side into the main part of the barn. There was an old threshing machine, a broken-down tractor and a hay wagon with flat tires. Looking around for a ladder to the loft, she saw another door. She opened it and pulled it two or three inches before it stuck on a high spot on the floor. She pulled harder, but it wouldn't move. It was too dark to see what was inside. Overcome with curiosity, she went in search of something to pry it open. As she did, she found the ladder in a dark corner.

She climbed quickly to the loft, but was disappointed to find it empty. It was very warm up there. She crossed to the side over the horse stalls and looked down the opening over the manger.

"Hi Starlight!" she shouted. "I'm up here."

Starlight nickered and looked around, apparently puzzled at hearing her voice.

"Don't worry, I'll be down soon."

Before going back down the ladder, Miranda circled the loft, just to make sure she didn't miss anything. On the side opposite the horse stalls, she found a small opening in the floor. She lay on her stomach and peered into the darkness below. There was another ladder leading down into the room with the stuck door. She climbed down.

Her foot struck something metal. Looking down, she saw the roof of an old car and stepped onto it. She was surprised to find that the room was full. The looters hadn't found this place. Maybe they had tried the door and given up. She climbed off the car and looked at it. It was in very good condition. So were the small tractor and mower that stood next to it. Miranda saw the outline of a door, big enough to drive a car through. She wondered why no one had come in that way. This room was only wide enough for the car and tractor, but there might be something in front of them.

The only light in the room came from the hayloft, but Miranda's eyes were adjusting to the dimness well enough to make out the shape of something covered with a canvas tarp. Dust choked her as she tugged on the heavy tarp. She tried again, holding her breath, and managed to fold it back to reveal a wheel with shiny spokes and a narrow rubber tire. Excitedly she pulled the tarp farther back, revealing a beautiful two-wheeled cart, with shafts made for a horse. Nothing was missing. The seat, wide enough for two people, was made of polished wood and padded with a black leather cover.

"This is way better than the one at Caruthers' sale!" Miranda exclaimed.

After caressing the wood and examining the shiny metal rings on the shaft, Miranda looked further. A rectangular wooden box, about six feet long an two feet wide, sat on the floor right behind the cart, also covered with the tarp. She tried to open it but it was locked.

Miranda climbed back up the ladder, ran across the hayloft and scurried down the other one. She circled the barn to find the door she had seen from the inside. The part of the barn she had been in was a shorter structure, adjoining the big barn. She went to where the door had to be, but there was nothing there but a solid wall. She hurried back to Starlight. He must be getting thirsty by now. She led him to the water trough and watched him drink.

"I'm going to put you back in the barn for now. I'll be back later, and we'll go to the racetrack. But right now, I've got to go get Mr. Taylor!"

Mr. Taylor was on the phone when Miranda burst into the house. She got a drink of water. Mr. Taylor motioned her away, as he began dialing again.

"But, Mr. Taylor, I . . ."

"Hello?" Mr. Taylor said into the phone, waving Miranda away. "Yes, I want to reinstate my entry in next week's races. Sir Jet Propelled Cadillac . . . yes, Colton Spencer . . . Yep, the horse is back in fine health. He'll be ready by race day."

Chapter Sixteen

Miranda was stunned. Next week? What was Mr. Taylor thinking? She hadn't even ridden Starlight yet.

"Mr. Taylor. You surely don't mean to race Starlight! Sure he's eating again, but he's weak. You can count every rib from a mile away, he's so thin!" Miranda exclaimed.

"Don't get all excited. I know what I'm doing. The way he's eating now, he'll be back in shape in no time. I want you to start riding him tomorrow. Not too much at first, but trot him around the track a few times. See how he does. I need the money from that race. I need it soon or I'll lose this ranch and Shady Hills too."

"What if he gets really sick from being pushed too hard?"

"We can always withdraw at the last minute if he isn't ready," Mr. Taylor said, "but I think he'll be fine."

Mr. Taylor was reaching for his hat and opening

the door before Miranda remembered why she'd come to the house.

"Oh, Mr. Taylor. You've got to come see what I found in the barn!" Miranda exclaimed.

"I don't have time for games," Mr. Taylor said, "I have business to take care of."

"Please, Mr. Taylor. It's not a game. Did you know that not everything was stolen? You have a nice car and tractor and the most beautiful little buggy in the barn!"

Mr. Taylor stopped and stared at her.

"Show me," he said.

Miranda took him first to the outside of the barn where the door should be, but wasn't.

"It's behind that wall, but the only way to get to it is to go through the hayloft," Miranda said.

Instead of following her, Mr. Taylor went to the corner and stared at the ends of the boards.

"Get me a crowbar," he said. "There's one in the garage on the bench in front of the pickup."

Miranda ran off, but came back in two minutes.

"It's locked, Mr. Taylor," she said.

"What's . . .? Oh the garage door, here." He pulled keys from his pocket, found the right one and handed it to her.

As soon as Miranda handed the bar to Mr. Taylor, he began prying off boards.

"My father must have nailed these on. Whenever he did something, he did a thorough job of it," Mr. Taylor said. "That's why I couldn't understand how this place got so run down. He must have been sick for a long time before he died."

Miranda heard a quaver in Mr. Taylor's voice and looked up at him. A tear spilled down his cheek. He looked very old in that moment, and Miranda started toward him. He wiped a tear from his face and went back to prying off boards.

"Go get Colton," he ordered, gruffly.

Colton looked up from the fence he was mending when she called. Lucky pulled his head from a hole he was digging and ran toward Miranda. She petted him until a rabbit caught his attention and he ran off, barking wildly.

Miranda watched the two men struggle with the boards, prying and pounding until she could see a sliding door behind it. It was closed and she couldn't see anything wrong with it. There were still many boards to take off, and she grew impatient. She went through the hayloft and climbed down into the room. With some of the boards off, a little more light shone through the cracks in the door. She looked around for more treasures.

She opened the door on the passenger side of the car. The other door was too close to the wall. There was plastic on the seats, but it hadn't kept rats or mice from getting in. The car reeked of droppings, and there were fuzzy mouse nests under the dash. Miranda closed the door and went to look at the tractor. It had a metal seat, so it had fared better. She climbed up, sat down and clutched the steering wheel. In front of the tractor, two eyes flashed in the dim outline of the cart. Miranda jumped down and tiptoed toward them. A large cat slunk away and disappeared under a wall. As Miranda walked back past the cart, she heard a faint mew.

She was just reaching into a nest under the seat of the cart when Mr. Taylor slid the door open far enough to let light in, revealing four tiny kittens. She picked one up for a better look. It was a calico-and-white ball of fur.

"I can't believe my eyes!" Mr. Taylor exclaimed as he wandered through the room, touching each item.

"The things I treasured most as a boy are in this barn. I thought they probably sold them all as soon as I left home. This was my first car. I bought it with my own hard-earned money, even though they were against me having it. Look at it, Colton. My dream car! A 1932 REO. Whew! It's going to need some cleaning up and new upholstery," he added as he closed the door.

"This little Farmall Cub is the tractor I used to mow the acres of lawn. Dad bought it for me when I was twelve, but made me keep track of the hours I worked to pay for it. He paid me fifty cents an hour," Mr. Taylor continued.

"Look over here, Mr. Taylor. This is the most darling little cart I've ever seen!"

"Well, well, well," Mr. Taylor said, coming around the tractor. "I got that for my tenth birthday, and a pony to go with it. I had a lot of fun until the pony spooked, ran off, and threw me out. My mother refused to let me drive it again after that. The cart disappeared and I never knew what happened to it." He took a step backward. "Well, I'll be . . . what's this?"

Miranda turned to see Mr. Taylor staring down at the long wooden box that was locked.

"I've got to find the key to this!" he exclaimed, and headed for the house. Miranda followed, but when he gave up looking for it, she went back to Starlight.

When Miranda came into the home stretch of the racetrack the next morning, she was surprised to see Mr. Taylor standing there with his stopwatch. She had risen early from her bed beside Starlight. She had groomed and walked him before bridling him and riding him to the track. She hadn't expected to see anyone for at least another hour. The sun was a bright red ball, just rising from the horizon.

"You're up early," Mr. Taylor said. "Glad to see you're getting ready for the race."

"I'm just riding for the fun, Mr. Taylor. I think it's too soon to start running him."

"Looks to me like he wants to," Mr. Taylor observed.

It was true that Starlight was literally champing at the bit, pulling the reins by stretching his neck and raising his nose. It took all her concentration to hold him in and try to relax him.

"Just let him canter a little. I'm not asking you to push him," Mr. Taylor said. "Wait. Where's your helmet?"

"Oh, I forgot," Miranda said, touching her bare head. "It's in my bag in the house."

"Jump down and go get it," Mr. Taylor demanded. "I'll put a saddle on so you don't fall off."

"I wouldn't fall off!" Miranda exclaimed, as she slid from Starlight's back.

"Nonetheless, we're going to take precautions. Your mother will hold me accountable."

When Miranda was back on Starlight in Colton's racing saddle, Mr. Taylor stood back and told her to let Starlight have his way.

"Won't it make him worse to run? We ought to work up to it gradually."

"Just see what he wants to do; he won't hurt

himself,"Mr. Taylor said. "We'll be careful."

Miranda shifted her weight slightly forward, letting the reins go slack. Starlight started at a trot. Miranda sat back, but Starlight picked up the pace and soon stretched into a canter. Miranda didn't fight him, partly because of Mr. Taylor's orders, but also because she was lost in the feeling she always experienced when she raced him, the feeling that they were one. Faster and faster he went. Miranda leaned over his neck and whispered, "You are the wind, Starlight. You and I are the wind."

"Keep going!" Mr. Taylor shouted when they dashed past him.

"Easy, boy. Don't hurt yourself for the old man," Miranda murmured to Starlight.

But Starlight didn't seem to be straining. He wanted to run. Miranda sat back and began pulling him in after they passed Mr. Taylor again. She finally slowed him to a walk in the backstretch and stopped in front of Mr. Taylor at the starting line.

"Two minutes and seven seconds," Mr. Taylor shouted. "That's all I wanted to know. He wasn't even trying and would have beaten many of the horses around here at that speed. By keeping up with the good nutrition and exercise, he'll be ready for Sam Houston."

"What do you mean?"

"The horse races in Houston. They start the twenty-fourth, nothing Christmas day, but races on the twenty-sixth and twenty-seventh. Starlight will race all three days."

"That's only two days away!"

"I know. We'll be traveling a couple hours tomorrow. But don't worry. The horse van is like a palace. He'll have all the room he wants and plenty of good food. You'll have plenty of time to get him acclimated and comfortable. You ride him on the track here, and Colton can start riding when we get to the track tomorrow evening. As long as you're around, I'm sure he'll run."

"Mr. Taylor, don't you care about Starlight? He's thin. He needs time to get in shape. Why are you in such a hurry?"

"We'll see how he's feeling. I'll even have a vet check him out at the track. I won't run him if it's going to endanger his health."

It took two and a half hours to drive through the morning traffic to the Sam Houston Race Park, giving Miranda plenty of time to think. She thought about Margot and Sea Foam. She could tell that Margot missed her a lot when she talked to her on the phone. Wouldn't it be nice to have a surprise for her when she returned?

"Mr. Taylor, what are you going to do with that little cart in the barn?"

"I'll take it back to Shady Hills when I go, I suppose, unless I have to sell it."

"Sell it! Why would you do that?"

"Miranda, things haven't been going as well as I hoped. When I heard I'd inherited this ranch, I supposed I could sell it for enough to get Shady Hills free and clear and have money left over to buy some more stock and equipment."

"But I thought you had lots of money!" Miranda exclaimed.

"Well, I made a couple of investments that didn't turn out well. I'm not the only one with financial troubles in these hard times," he said gruffly.

"Sorry, I just didn't know," Miranda said.

"Well, I suppose not. Kids aren't supposed to have to worry about such things," Mr. Taylor said, more gently. "Anyway, it was a big disappointment to see that this place was so run down, and an even bigger one to find out that it was mortgaged to the hilt! My parents were so far in debt, it would have been impossible to pay it all off even if the place had been in tiptop shape. It makes me sick to see that all the expensive antiques and equipment were stolen or damaged."

"Except for your buggy and stuff," Miranda said.

"Yeah. Now that was something I never expected. I had no idea they'd save my things. They were so mad at me when I left, they said they didn't want to see me again. I took them at their word and never called or came back to see them." Mr. Taylor's voice cracked and he wiped a tear from his face.

Miranda sat quietly, understanding that he was embarrassed to cry in her and Colton's presence.

"Don't ever make that mistake, either one of you. No matter what happens, or how mad you get at your parents, don't hold a grudge. Talk things out while there's still time."

"Did you ever find the key to the box?"

"Not yet. I'm going to get a locksmith to open it when I get back to the ranch. It's a very intricate lock built into the wood. I hate to break into it."

"I looked at the workmanship on that box, Mr. Taylor," Colton said. "Someone took a lot of time and care making it. It sure isn't factory-made."

"I made it for my mother when I took woodworking in high school. I thought she could use it for storing her fine linens. She was so proud of her beautiful tablecloths and she had the most beautiful wedding gown that she wanted to keep. She'd hoped to let my bride wear it someday. But she didn't approve of my choice of a wife. I never knew what happened to it, but she didn't even show it to Jesse."

"Maybe it's still in the box!" Miranda exclaimed.

"I doubt it. Mother didn't like the box and refused to use it. She made me put it in the barn, where she would never have to look at it. She said it looked like a coffin and she wasn't going to have it in her bedroom," Mr. Taylor said, bitterness sharpening his voice. "I made it long and narrow to set at the foot of her bed. It's lined with cedar. I carved the top of it with a picture of the ranch and I engraved her name in it. She accused me of wishing her dead."

"Oh, Mr. Taylor! How terrible! How could she say such things after all the love and hard work you put into it?"

Chapter Seventeen

The Sam Houston Race Park was bustling with excitement. Mr. Taylor let Miranda take care of Starlight while he set up their sleeping quarters and took care of some "business." Miranda led Starlight around the stable area, past horses on exercise wheels, to the racetrack. When she got to the track, she saw that it was empty except for a few riders on horseback walking or jogging around it. Starlight's ears pricked forward and his body tensed as he watched the horses on the track.

"You love racing, don't you, Starlight? You want to join them?" Miranda asked, knowing the answer already. "Okay. I just have to go put a bridle and saddle on you and get my helmet."

Miranda started Starlight at a walk, away from other horses, then she let him trot. When another horse cantered past them, Starlight jumped forward, catching up very quickly and keeping pace. The rider glanced at her, and then looked again to stare in surprise. Miranda smiled as Starlight surged past them.

She didn't let him go faster than a jog the second time around. People stared at her, but she ignored them, concentrating on Starlight, making sure he didn't get too tired. At the end of that lap, she took him back to the pickup and horse van. It had been decided that he would stay in it, rather than a stall in the stables. Miranda could put her sleeping bag on the ledge that served as a feeder over the tack compartment.

True to his word, Mr. Taylor had a veterinarian examine Starlight the next morning.

"He's thin, but sound. I don't think one race a day is going to hurt him," he said.

At post time, Miranda stood with Mr. Taylor near the fence even with the finish line. The horses would cross it twice, once after leaving the gate, and again after rounding the track. She stretched to see the starting gate. As it opened, Starlight surged ahead of the pack. Colton made no effort to hold him back, and he was a length ahead by the time he thundered past Miranda. Mr. Taylor nudged her and smiled.

"See?" he shouted. "He's in fine form. Up to his usual performance. This one's in the bag!"

But Miranda was climbing the fence to see the far side of the track. Starlight, now leading by almost three lengths, had slowed. Colton sat relaxed in the saddle, for experience had shown them that Starlight would speed up on his own when other horses came into his view. As a horse came up on the inside, Starlight seemed to slow a little more, turning his head slightly to the left as if to greet the horse. A horse on the outside was now just half a length behind Starlight, who seemed to slow even more until it was beside him.

"Now, Colton," Miranda whispered. "Tell him to go!"

As if he had heard her, Colton rose up in the saddle and leaned over Starlight's neck. Starlight's left ear went back as if he were listening to Colton. Yet he didn't surge ahead. He seemed to have lost interest. In fact, he was looking toward the outer rail. Colton, standing in the stirrups, leaned farther forward, moving his hands back and forth on Starlight's neck. He didn't carry a crop, as most riders did, for Starlight had never needed prodding.

Mr. Taylor was jumping up and down, shouting at Colton and Starlight, who, of course, could not hear him.

"What's the matter with him?" he asked Miranda. "He's quitting on us. Why?"

Miranda didn't know she was at the top of the fence screaming at Starlight herself, ignoring the onlookers who were telling her to get down. Starlight, now only a few yards from the finish line, pricked up his ears and cut across the track toward Miranda. He streaked past two horses and crossed the finish line in second place before coming to a jolting halt in front of Miranda.

Mr. Taylor threw his hat to the ground in disgust, but Miranda jumped into the track and ran to her horse.

"Sorry, Miranda. He just didn't listen to me,"

Colton said, stepping down.

"Get that kid off the track!" someone yelled from the crowd.

"Boost me up, Colton," Miranda ordered. Colton did so and then led Starlight off the track.

"He isn't even sweating! Do you think he's tired?" Miranda asked. "He's not limping, is he?"

"He seems to be fine," Colton said.

Mr. Taylor met them as they left the track and headed for the trailer. He walked beside Colton and didn't say anything for a long time. Miranda waited, feeling his anger and disappointment as if she were somehow responsible.

"Tomorrow's a holiday," Mr. Taylor began.

Duh, it's Christmas, Miranda thought, suddenly realizing how strange that felt. She hadn't bought any presents. She had planned to do all her shopping in the few free days of school vacation before Christmas.

"I want only Colton to ride Starlight on the track tomorrow," Mr. Taylor said. "Miranda, you can try sitting in the grandstand or standing by the fence. We'll see if that helps him or distracts him. Then we will have you leave, and see if he does any better without you anywhere around."

Starlight's time on the trial runs didn't please Mr. Taylor. He was fast, possibly fast enough to come in first, but not if anything went wrong, or if he decided he didn't care about winning. Miranda wished Mr. Taylor would give up. By the third time around the track, he showed signs of tiring.

"Okay, that's enough," Mr. Taylor said, before walking away. "Let Miranda cool him down."

Miranda called home and wished everyone a merry Christmas. She heard all about the gifts they'd each received and how much fun Kort had with the wrapping paper and boxes. They told Miranda they missed her and wished she were there.

"I can't wait until you get home," Margot said. "There's a whole pile of presents here with your name on them. But there's one surprise I can give you now! I asked if I could tell you, and Mom said yes."

"What? It must be good news. Is it about Sea Foam?"

"No, but she's doing fine. I spend time with her every day."

"Tell me!" Miranda said. "What's the surprise?"

"We're going to have a new baby sister or brother next August. Mom's pregnant!"

Starlight's race was at ten o'clock on the morning after Christmas. Starlight was antsy. Mr. Taylor decided it would be better for Miranda to stay out of sight until after the race. It was all she could do to stay away, but she watched the race on a monitor inside the building. Again Starlight started ahead of the pack, but began to lag after passing the grandstand. Yet he stayed slightly ahead and was neck and neck with two other horses as they entered the backstretch. Miranda watched Colton lean forward and knew he was talking to him. Starlight flicked an ear backward, but instead of surg-

ing ahead as he had done in races in Montana and California, he abruptly slowed down. A horse directly behind him actually ran into him, and Starlight put his ears back. By then the race was over and Starlight crossed the finish line in fifth place.

Miranda ran to where Colton would come off the track. Mr. Taylor wasn't there, much to Miranda's relief. He would not be in a good mood! Colton, leading Starlight from the track, shook his head when he saw her. Starlight reached out and nudged her with his nose.

"Starlight, I guess you aren't as crazy about racing as I thought you were," Miranda said. "Well, it's all right by me. Now maybe Mr. Taylor will just let you go home and stay there."

"I rode him just like you showed me, Miranda. Just like I did in California and all the other races he's won," Colton said. "I just don't understand what's gotten into him."

"I don't think it's your fault, Colton. Maybe he's tired. You know how sick he was!"

"He isn't even sweating," Colton said.

"Watch out, here comes Mr. Taylor."

"Let's load up. We're going home," Mr. Taylor said. "I've withdrawn from tomorrow's race."

"You mean home to Montana?" Miranda asked.

"No, back to the my parents' ranch. I'll go see an attorney in the morning about filing Chapter Eleven. I hoped to win some money here but I just got myself deeper in debt. We'll let the banks have the ranches."

Mr. Taylor looked old and defeated. His face was a wall of pain, and he wouldn't look anyone in the eye.

"What's Chapter Eleven?"

"Bankruptcy!" Mr. Taylor snarled.

"Do you mean you have to give up Shady Hills as well as your parent's ranch?" Miranda asked in alarm.

"It means I can't pay my bills, so I lose everything. I'll be lucky if they let me keep Sir Jet."

"Mr. Taylor, we can't let them have Starlight. He's mine . . . well, half mine. You signed a paper so no one else could buy him."

"It's not my call!" Mr. Taylor shouted. "I'll talk to the attorney tomorrow. Now get Starlight loaded," he added in a softer tone.

Chapter Eighteen

Miranda couldn't say another word, for a painful lump of sorrow blocked her throat. She blinked back tears as she clutched Starlight's halter and continued walking.

"Hey Cash!" someone shouted. "I have a wager for you."

Miranda saw a middle-aged man striding toward him.

"I don't have anything to bet, Edward, I'm done," Mr. Taylor said, moving along.

"Wait!" Edward said, jogging to catch up. "I just want you to put your money where your mouth is, and if you don't have money, how about your horse?"

"What do you want?" Mr. Taylor asked angrily when the man grabbed his arm.

"I listened to you brag up that horse saying he could beat anything, and when he loses twice in a row, you walk off owing me money," the man said, not letting go of Mr. Taylor's arm. "I want to know how and when I'm going to get the money you bet me. Your parting shot was that if Miranda had been riding he'd have won. I don't know who Miranda is, but I'll wager that you're wrong. It's your chance to get your money back. And if you lose, I get the horse."

"No way!" Miranda shouted. "He's half mine, Mr. Taylor!"

"She's right," Mr. Taylor said. "Now let go of me, Edward!"

"Who's this?" Edward asked, reaching for Miranda. She pulled away.

"This is Miranda Stevens. This horse belongs to her."

"All right, you have other horses, and you owe me money. If Miranda wins, I'll cancel your debt. If I win, I can come to your Montana ranch and pick out any horse I want."

"Miranda can't race. She's a little girl! Are you blind?"

"This evening, after the races, she can run against the clock and if she beats the time of the winner of the race that Starlight just lost, you'll win. If not, I do."

"How about tomorrow morning, eight o'clock?" Mr. Taylor asked. "And for every fifth of a second better than the winning time, you pay a thousand dollars."

"You're greedy, Taylor, but you're on. I'll see you in the morning."

Miranda couldn't believe her ears. She argued with Mr. Taylor, and so did Colton.

"You're putting a lot on Miranda, Mr. Taylor. We don't know if Starlight can do it. He's still thin. He hasn't run that fast since he left Montana. Maybe he can't anymore."

"Stay out of this, Colton. I have a lot at stake here," Mr. Taylor said. "Miranda, if you don't want to do this, we'll load up right now and go back to the ranch. I'll call my attorney and file Chapter 11. You can go back to Montana and I'll try to bring Starlight back after it's all settled, but it will be up to the courts.

Miranda and Starlight were on the track before seven. After walking around the track once, Miranda got off and stood in front of Starlight.

"I love you, Starlight," she said when he pressed his face against her. "Mr. Taylor needs us, today. I hate to ask you, but do you think you could run like you did for me in Montana? But if it's going to be bad for you, I don't want you to. You're worth more than all the money in the world, and I don't want to hurt you. But I don't want to lose you either."

Tears fell as she leaned her head against his forehead. When he lifted his head, she stepped back.

"Good to see you up so early," Mr. Taylor said. "Let's do a practice run, and I'll time it. If he isn't up to speed, we can still leave."

"No! I'm not running him more than once. He isn't as strong as he was. If you don't believe in him, why did you tell the man you'd race?"

"Sorry, Miranda. Colton's right. I'm putting too much on you — and too much on Starlight. I just hate to lose everything, and it's making me desperate. Do you want to go home?"

"You gave your word. I don't see how we can," Miranda said, looking at Starlight. "Besides, I think Starlight can beat two minutes, three and two-fifth seconds. That's what won yesterday, right?"

Mr. Taylor nodded.

The sparkle of excitement was back in Starlight's eyes. Though terribly thin, he seemed strong and full of life. Miranda kept him at a slow trot as they warmed up. Coming around the track she heard Edward's booming voice.

"Well, well, well. I hardly expected you to show, Taylor. You must really believe in this horse."

In the starting gate Miranda tried not to transfer her fears to Starlight. She was more nervous than she had ever been. When the gate opened Starlight surged forward as Miranda leaned over his neck and held on. The thrill of the speed, the sense of being one with the horse, with the wind, and something bigger than both of them, made Miranda forget everything but the joy of the ride.

"Yee haw, Starlight, I love you!" she screamed in sheer delight.

Starlight stretched his stride and quickened his pace, eating up the track in another burst of speed. As they thundered past a crowd of people at the finish line, Miranda giggled and sat back in the saddle.

Colton was in the track jumping up and down when they came around again and stopped in front of the crowd.

"You did it! Two minutes, fifty nine and one-fifth seconds," he shouted.

"Where did all these people come from?" Miranda asked as she let Colton help her down.

"Mr. Taylor rounded them up this morning and

got them to bet against Starlight," Colton said. "I think you may have saved the ranch, Miranda."

"Not me," Miranda said. "Starlight."

"He couldn't do it without you," Colton said. "I like to think I'm a pretty good rider, but it took you to give him the heart to do it."

"Me and Starlight," Miranda said. "We are a winning team!"

"Did we make enough to save both ranches, Mr. Taylor?" Miranda asked as they drove into the Texas ranch.

"It was a good start, Miranda. I have enough to pay the back taxes on this place, and make a pretty good dent in the debt to the nursing home, and some other creditors. I'm hoping I can sell it for enough to pay most of it."

"What about Shady Hills?"

"That's another story," Mr. Taylor said with a sigh. "I need to keep racing horses, especially Starlight, in order to pay the mortgage on it."

Miranda was in a somber mood when they arrived back at the ranch, but she couldn't help but smile as Lucky, who Mr. Taylor had insisted be left behind, bounded to meet them with a doggy grin and happy whine. Miranda determined to spend every possible minute with Starlight in the last three days she had before she had to fly back to Montana; but when she came in to get a drink of water, she found Mr. Taylor poring over racing schedules, planning a tour that would take

Starlight east, farther from home than ever.

"But he'll get sick again. I don't think Mom will let me go with you."

"I've thought of that. But I think he'll do okay with Colton for a while at least," Mr. Taylor said, rubbing his eyes. "I don't know any other way, unless I sell Shady Hills, too. Maybe that's what I should do."

Miranda slid down in a chair and stared at the ceiling, as she felt Mr. Taylor's despair added to her own.

"What's that?" she asked suddenly.

"What?"

"Up above the cupboard by the ceiling. It looks like a little door."

Mr. Taylor looked to where she pointed.

"Oh, for heaven's sake!" Mr. Taylor exclaimed. "I forgot all about that. My dad put that little compartment in there when he built the kitchen cabinets. He said it was our little joke. He said we'd see how long it took for Mom to notice it was there. She was a short woman and never used the top shelves of the cupboards, except for things she rarely used. Then she had Dad or me get them down or put them up for her."

Mr. Taylor was pushing a chair up to the cupboard. He had to stand on the countertop to reach the little door. It was stuck.

"There's a screwdriver in my tool box on the porch, Miranda. Would you get it for me?"

He jammed the screwdriver blade under the edge of the door and pried. After he did this in three places the door sprang open. He reached inside.

"Empty," he said. "No, wait a minute. One of

Dad's tobacco cans is pushed way to the back. He hid his vices from Mother."

He climbed down and set the can on the table and returned to his race schedules. Miranda was curious about the rusty narrow tin can with the hinged lid. She picked it up and shook it. It rattled. She opened the lid and turned it upside down. A key clattered onto the table.

"That's it!" Mr. Taylor exclaimed. "That's the key to the cedar chest I made for Mother. Come on. Let's go open it."

The first thing Miranda saw in the box was a small Western saddle. Beneath that were a harness, bridles, and halters.

"This is all the tack I had for my pony. She was half Welsh and half Arabian, bigger than most ponies, so my father had these custom-made to fit her. I was sure he'd sold them after Mother told me I couldn't keep the pony!"

They took each item out and examined it. Everything was in perfect condition; no mice, sun, or moisture could get into this well-constructed box. As Miranda oohed over the tack, laying it out on the seat of the cart where the light was better, Mr. Taylor continued to rummage inside.

"Look," he shouted. "My twenty-two!"

He held up a small rifle, grinning like a child on Christmas morning. He handed it to Colton, and went back to the box, pulling out a pair of cowboy boots, a pair of chaps, and a wide-brimmed hat that looked like it would fit Kort.

"Just one more thing," he said. "Looks like a picture album."

Miranda immediately dropped what she was doing to look at the pictures of Mr. Taylor's childhood. She squealed over the cute little guy dressed in the very boots, chaps, and hat they'd just found. He was sitting on a horse in front of a man who looked a lot like Mr. Taylor, only younger.

"There I am with my father. He looks pretty proud and happy, doesn't he?" Mr. Taylor sounded surprised when he said this.

There were two more pages of pictures, and then nothing but old papers and documents. Mr. Taylor walked to the door where the light was better. Miranda went back to laying out the harness, trying to figure out exactly how it would go on a horse.

"Yeeeeee-haww, I'll be a monkey's fat uncle!" Mr. Taylor shouted.

Both Colton and Miranda jumped, and then stared as if they feared the old man had totally lost his mind.

"What's the matter, Mr. Taylor?" Miranda asked, running to his side.

"Matter? Nothing. Nothing at all. We just saved the ranches. Both of them. Thanks, Dad. Thank you."

Mr. Taylor dropped to his knees and tears streamed down his face. Miranda looked at Colton. He looked as scared as she felt. They both looked back at Mr. Taylor sitting on the ground next to the building, He opened the album that he'd been clutching to his breast.

"Mr. Taylor?" Colton asked tentatively.

"It's all right, kids," Mr. Taylor said. "I'm sorry if I scared you. You see, when I was a youngster my father bought a lot of stock in major oil companies and utilities, as well as savings bonds. He put some of them in my name. At the time, I thought it was just to keep from paying taxes. But here they are, all of them. And worth a hundred times more than what Dad paid for them. Kids, I have enough to bail out both ranches, with money left over. Let's go back to Montana."

If you enjoyed *Miranda and Starlight,*
Starlight's Courage, Starlight, Star Bright,
Starlight's Shooting Star and
Starlight Shines for Miranda,
you'll want to read the exciting conclusion
to the saga of Miranda Stevens
and her beloved horse, Starlight.
Book 6, *Starlight Comes Home,*
will be available in late 2004.

Ask for these books
in your favorite book store
or purchase them directly from the publisher.
Ordering information on back of this page.

Happy Reading and Riding to You!

Send check or money order to:
Raven Publishing
P.O. Box 2885
Norris, MT 59745
$9.00 per book plus $2.00 shipping and handling for one
and $.50 for each additional book.
Or order on line at *www.ravenpublishing.net*
For more information, e-mail:
info@ravenpublishing.net
Phone: *406-685-3545*
Toll Free: 866-685-3545
Fax: *406-685-3599*

Name_____

Address_____

City_____State_____Zip_____

Please send me:
_____copies of **Miranda and Starlight**

_____copies of **Starlight's Courage**

_____copies of **Starlight, Star Bright**

_____copies of **Starlight's Shooting Star**

_____copies of **Starlight Shines for Miranda**

Starlight Comes Home (Available after 11/2004)

Ask for these books
in your favorite book store
or purchase them directly from the publisher.
Ordering information on back of this page.

Happy Reading and Riding to You!

Send check or money order to:
Raven Publishing
P.O. Box 2885
Norris, MT 59745
$9.00 per book plus $2.00 shipping and handling for one
and $.50 for each additional book.
Or order on line at *www.ravenpublishing.net*
For more information, e-mail:
info@ravenpublishing.net
Phone: *406-685-3545*
Toll Free: 866-685-3545
Fax: *406-685-3599*

Name _AVERY N. BROOKS_____

Address_____

City_____State _OHIO_ Zip_____

Please send me:
_____copies of **Miranda and Starlight**

_____copies of **Starlight's Courage**

_____copies of **Starlight, Star Bright**

_____copies of **Starlight's Shooting Star**

_____copies of **Starlight Shines for Miranda**

Starlight Comes Home (Available after 11/2004)